AFRICAN WRITERS SERIES LIST
Founding editor · Chinua Achebe

AFRICAN WRITERS SERIES

143

Kill Me Quick

Kill Me Quick

MEJA MWANGI

HEINEMANN
LONDON . NAIROBI . IBADAN

Heinemann Educational Books Ltd
48 Charles Street, London W1X 8AH
P.M.B. 5205, Ibadan · P.O. Box 45314, Nairobi ·
P.O. Box 3966, Lusaka
EDINBURGH MELBOURNE TORONTO AUCKLAND
SINGAPORE HONG KONG KUALA LUMPUR NEW DELHI

ISBN 0 435 90143 5

Printed by Cox & Wyman Ltd
London, Fakenham and Reading

Days run out for me,
Life goes from bad to worse,
Very soon, very much soon,
Time will lead me to the end.
Very well. So be it.
But one thing I beg of you.
If the sun must set for me,
If all must come to an end,
If you must be rid of me,
The way you have done with all my friends,
If you must kill me,
Do so fast.
KILL ME QUICK.

This little book is dedicated to all those little Mejas still in the back streets of the city, destined to stay there until they come of age, when the green van will come and whisk them off to Number Nine.

1

MEJA SAT BY the ditch swinging his legs this way and that. A few people passed by engrossed in their daily problems and none of them gave the lanky youth a thought. But the searching eyes of Meja missed nothing. They scrutinised the ragged beggars who floated ghostly past him as closely as they watched the smart pot-bellied executives wrinkling their noses at the foul stench of the backyards. And between these two types of beings, Meja made comparisons.

Then Maina came out of the back gate of the supermarket and Meja's thoughts were diverted to his friend. He ran over and helped him carry the heavy parcels back to the trench. There in the empty parking lot by the ditch, they unwrapped the bundles and Meja gazed glassy-eyed at their prize. There were various kinds of fruit in various stages of decay. There were also slices of stale, smelly bread and a few pieces of dusty chocolate. Some rock-hard cakes glared stonily back at them. Meja sat looking from one type of food to the other. The oranges were no longer orange and beautiful but a deathly grey with mould. The cakes were no longer cakes but fragments of rock, and the chocolate looked like discarded shoe polish.

'Let's eat,' Maina said and his hand dived into the food.

Meja was a fraction of a moment slower in responding, but soon they were munching and chewing hungrily. And between mouthfuls of food, they talked. Maina did most of the talking and Meja listened as patiently as ever.

'I came out here raw and proud the way you are,' Maina said to Meja scraping away the rotten side of an orange. 'I thought I would get a job and earn six–seven hundred shillings a month. Then I would get a house, a radio, good clothes and food.' He paused.

He cracked a piece of cake by throwing it hard to the ground and handed Meja a piece. Meja put it into his mouth and bit hard but the cake would not break. Maina was already crunching his piece and enjoying the meal greatly. He glanced at Meja and picked another piece of cake.

'Well, I tried to get a job,' he said and shrugged. "What qualifications?" they would ask me. "Second Division School Cert. . . ." I would start to say but before I had finished the man behind the desk would roar, "Get out, we have no jobs."'

He tasted a bit of the sticky chocolate and handed it to Meja.

Meja shook his head and stared blankly back at his friend. A few yards away people passed. Occasionally one of the passers-by glanced in their direction, saw nothing unusual about two youths sitting by the gutter eating oranges, and continued minding his own business.

'I don't blame you for having a soft stomach,' Maina said taking a big bite of the chocolate. 'I wouldn't touch the stuff myself when I first came out here. I lived like a god, on porridge and posho. But there was no job for anybody, anywhere. The same story everywhere. "Qualifications? Get out." "Second Division," I would start to say before they banged the door shut.'

He cut the bread in two and handed his friend a piece. Meja tried to eat it and almost vomited trying. Maina watched and shook his head in disapproval.

'Try an orange,' he advised.

Meja followed instructions and decided the orange was not very bad apart from the smell. He held his breath every time he brought the orange to his face to take a bite and reduced the smell problem considerably.

'So,' Maina went on, 'all my friends became thieves and robbers. I would have done the same too but I was too cowardly to break into houses at night. I had not done much practice in running at school and could never trust my speed for getting away with purse snatching. So my friends went into the main streets and snatched purses and they are almost all of them in prison now, for one reason or another. Me, I turned into the backstreets and thrived. There isn't much competition for existence here, except with the mongrels and mongrels do not know how to open closed back doors. And the food is not all that bad if you allow for the smell, and such minor things.'

He finished the last orange and wrapped the left-overs in old newspapers. He pushed the store under a nearby culvert. Meja watched him and nibbled at his third orange breathlessly.

'That was good,' Maina said licking his lips and belching loudly. 'What will you do now, son of Mwangi? Go back to the village?' He laughed softly and then became serious.

Meja twitched and looked away.

'No,' he said slowly.

'I am glad you won't,' Maina said thoughtfully, 'let me tell you Meja. I will be anything on this jobless earth, but any sort of worm never. Not again. I was the wormest sort of book-worm at school. Other boys laughed at me then because of the funny things I did with books. I carried a book everywhere, even into the dining hall. There was a day I bit the book instead of my food and you should have heard them laugh, Meja. It was terrible the way the story raced from mouth to mouth. There was also a time I carried a book into the toilet and read so as not to waste any time. After relieving myself, I threw the book into the basin and flushed the water. I nearly ran mad when I realised what I had done.' He sniggered and then sighed. 'So you see I am through with books. More than twelve years in school with fees to pay and then I go back home and just hang around; no not me, Meja. Imagine how my friends who never went to school and always stayed at home will laugh! I believe that I have a right to something better if only for the effort I put into those examination weeks. And what about the fees I had to pay at school? I could have become a farmer without having to pay all that highly, you know.' He stretched and yawned.

'What will you do?' he asked his friend.

Meja looked this way and that and tried to hide his confusion. He had been in the city for three days and he had not liked anything about it. The busy indifferent people, the multitude of vehicles and the huge buildings had all filled him with fear. To him it all seemed like a new strange world way out of the universe where every other human being was a rival, every car a charging beast and every building a mysterious castle. The idea of staying in this heartless place was terrifying, but then so was the idea of going back home without having found that job he came to seek.

'I will stick around a while and see if anything changes,' he said, studying his old shoes.

Maina pondered over the idea.

'Yes, do that,' he advised. 'There is no point in trying for a job, but do that. At least it will satisfy you.'

He stood deep in thought. Then he yawned again. 'Meet me here in the evening for supper. Then we can go to sleep.'

Meja Mwangi did not ask where they were going to sleep. Looking around the dirty backstreet strewn with dustbins he could already guess.

'Where are you going?' he asked Maina.

'Nowhere in particular,' the other said. 'Anywhere I can get a cigarette. That is about the only thing they don't provide for in the backstreets.'

Meja stood up and straightened his clothes. He was almost the same build as Maina, big bones and wide intelligent eyes. The only difference between the two youths was that while Meja was dressed in an old baggy black suit, a wide tie and a pair of oversize shoes that once belonged to his father, Maina was dressed in khaki shorts, now tattered and anything but khaki in colour, and his feet were bare and horny, the nails of the toes standing out at weird angles.

Looking up Meja saw the other staring at his clothes.

3

'Those clothes could fetch you a few shillings,' Maina said. 'Take good care of them. You might need the money.'

Meja nodded, feeling raw.

'And the shoes too,' Maina added and started walking away.

Then he stopped and looked back at Meja who stood undecided.

'Listen, Meja,' he said. 'If they tell you to get out, get out. Do so fast or they will throw you downstairs. I speak from experience. Also keep away from the mainstreets.'

Then he turned and went away.

Meja stood and for a little while digested what the veteran of the backstreets had told him. Like everything else in the city it sounded unreal and cruel. Yet, he felt in his heart that what he had been told was true. Those two, it seemed, were the simple rules for survival.

He walked for the whole day from office to office until his feet were tired and sore. He talked to anybody he thought might be able to help, from office boys to managers. Few wanted even to hear him sing out his qualifications or to know whether he had any. But undaunted he carried on. He repeated his piece in so many offices that he became addicted to it. He said it without thinking and this did not make matters any better. Late in the afternoon he went into a big office and found the manager and the secretary.

The manager, obviously sleepy from the effects of a heavy lunch, looked up lazily from his work. Meja looking his most humble, stood at the door and the two stared at one another for a moment. The manager was trying to focus his thoughts on the newcomer and the other waited for permission to speak. Then the manager woke up.

'Well, what do you want?' he asked.

Meja breathed hard and put on his most intelligent look in an effort to cover his misery.

'First Division School Certificate,' he announced.

The manager took his cigar from the corner of his lips, placed it on the ash tray, took off his spectacles next and then scrutinised Meja. He took the youth in slowly and deliberately, the way a scientist studies a specimen.

The secretary had paused with one hand on the spacing lever of her typewriter and the other poised undecidedly over the keys.

Then: 'Well, what about it?' the manager spoke to the young man.

Meja's heart faltered then recovered and hammered in his chest. He licked his lips.

'I . . . I want a job . . . vacancy,' he said.

The manager put his glasses back on, apparently satisfied that his adversary was harmless and stuck his cigar back at the corner of his lips. He chewed at it, sucked strongly and emitted a thick black cloud.

'How did you come in here?' he asked.

'I . . . I came,' Meja could not possibly guess what was expected of him.

'Through the main door, I presume,' the big man said.

Meja nodded and said a dry 'yes'.

'Can you read?' the man asked.

Hope soared through Meja. His voice trembled with ecstasy.

'Yes . . . yes,' he said. 'I can also write.'

'Then you ought to have written down your request,' the other said. 'Anyhow . . .'

He pressed a blue button on his desk. At this point the secretary threw him an ugly look and restarted her machine rattling. A messenger walked into the office and stood at attention.

'Go with him,' the manager said to Meja and went back to scanning some forms that needed signing.

Meja's thoughts were unfathomable as he followed the messenger down the many winding stairs. His mind raced ahead of him. A job at last. The two reached the ground floor and the huge glass doors. The messenger led him to the big doors and showed him the tiny white letters painted on one of the doors.

It took Meja one long minute to grasp the meaning of it all. And then he understood and could not believe. He could not believe that the messenger had gone to all that trouble to show him this. Yet the letters were there staring boldly back at him. They screamed in two tongues: NO VACANCY. HAKUNA KAZI.

Meja's legs felt wobbly and his lips twitched. He looked round for the messenger, but his job done, the other had vanished back into the bowels of the cold building.

Slowly his legs started moving away from the taunting notice. He was discouraged and desperate. He had to get a job at any price, for any price. Any sort of job. And now as he chased around for the job he was a little wiser. He would always first look for the insignificant little notice that hung on most doors and meant so much. As the day wore on he became more desperate. He started to even go into restaurants looking for a job as a sweeper but there was none anywhere. He made his services as cheap as thirty shillings per month but still nobody was interested.

He was crossing a backstreet to go into an Arab owned restaurant, to plead with the manager, when he came across his table-mate, Maina. He was carrying a huge carton which attracted a swarm of flies and they came screaming after him. The two boys stopped and stared at one another for a moment, one looking sad and weary and the other resigned and contented. Maina broke the silence.

'Do you care for a pie?' he asked reaching into the carton.

5

'No,' the other said quickly.

'Any luck?'

Meja shook his head and looked away up the street.

A rubbish truck came down the street emptying the dustbins and the two moved to one side to let it pass.

'You are going to the restaurant?' Maina asked.

Meja nodded.

'Good luck,' Maina said and started walking away.

'Maina,' Meja said and swallowed hard.

The other stopped and looked back.

'Come, Maina,' Meja said. 'Let us go together. I . . . I am afraid. Maybe they will pity us and give us a job if we go together. I don't want to go alone, Maina.'

Maina looked horrified. He looked at his frightened friend and his own tattered clothes. He shook his head.

'No, Meja,' he said. 'I can't. It will only make matters worse the way I am dressed.'

They stared at one another and Meja swallowed again painfully.

'You must go alone,' Maina told him. 'You might be lucky. I dare not go in there. Have courage, they will not kill you. If I go with you they won't even let us in.'

Meja nodded slowly. He understood. Maina could not help him. He had to face it alone. He turned and started walking towards the back door of the restaurant.

'And, Meja,' the other shouted after him.

He stopped.

'Tell them everything,' Maina told him. 'Tell them you had one points in . . . what was it?'

'Physics, Maths and Chemistry,' Meja told him.

'Yes, tell them, if you think it will help.'

He turned into another backstreet.

Meja dragged himself into the restaurant and met the manager. The man looked him up and down as was expected before talking to him.

'What do you want?' he asked.

'Job,' Meja said hopelessly.

The manager looked him up and down again.

'What sort of job can you do?' he asked.

'Any,' Meja said quickly.

'And what qualifications do you have?' the manager asked.

Meja took a deep breath and made sure to tell it the right way round. He was not going to mess up another opportunity.

'First Division, School Certificate, with one points in . . .' he bleated.

'That is not a qualification,' the manager cut him short. 'Everybody

6

has done and passed the examination. What I am asking for is experience.'

Meja's face fell and his legs felt weak. His stomach ached badly and he felt his tongue choking him.

'Ex – experience?' he stammered.

'Yes, experience,' the manager answered watching the wretched trembling figure. 'Points won't be much help in the kitchen. Well, what experience have you got? What can you cook?'

Meja made an effort to clear his mind of the feeling of hopelessness and dejection.

'I can cook posho and . . . and porridge,' he said.

'What is that?' the manager showed surprise.

Meja twitched and struggled with his thoughts. Fear was already creeping on him.

'I can also sweep and wash dishes and . . .' he whined, 'chop wood.'

'We don't use wood here.'

Meja's shoulders drooped. He tried to shrug but that came out too badly so he shook his head looking at the clean floor of the office.

The manager was becoming impatient.

'No vacancy,' he announced.

'But please, any job . . . thirty . . . twenty . . . anything you like,' he pleaded.

'I said there is no vacancy.'

'Please . . . please.'

'Ahmed,' the manager called into the adjoining office.

Meja knew that he was violating one of the major rules for survival but he stayed. He was determined to stay and never to go back into the backstreets with the mongrels. He felt that he belonged out here and this was where he was going to stay. He put up a resistance.

He was still shouting, 'Maths . . . first . . . chemistry . . . physics,' in confused order when they threw him out minus a few buttons and plus a few bruises here and there. It took two big bullies and the manager to toss him through the back door.

He rejoined Maina in very low spirits that evening. He felt ready to take a rope and end the suffering. He did not want to go back to the alleyways but after floating hopelessly around the city he decided there was no other place to go. So he slunk back hating everything and everybody. He made it a point to hate Maina too, together with his backstreets. Most of all he hated the cruel world which had no place for people with one points in maths, physics and chemistry. He would not touch the pies his friend put in front of him. That was a bad gesture after his friend had gone to all that trouble to get them.

'You will come off it,' Maina told him in low tones full of concern. 'Forget about your first division and learn to live with the world. It is

7

everybody for himself and to the devil with school certificate. You know what, Meja? I would not go back to school if they paid me to. What for? In the one year that I have been here I have learned that it does not pay. It has not got me anywhere.'

Meja glared back at him.

'And temper, Meja,' the other went on. 'Temper does not get you anywhere out here either. See what happened to your beautiful clothes. Nobody will even speak to you while you are dressed like that. Don't you ever let them see you in the mainstreets either. You will be pushed under so fast that you will take long to realise where you are.'

Then as Maina talked Meja understood what it was all about. As Maina put it they did not belong out there in the high streets with their big shops and neon lights. They had, by city standards, only enough education to know how to spell their first names. The choice was now either going into the mainstreets – and eventually to jail; or remaining in the backstreets and rotting there, though Maina called it thriving.

The evening passed slowly and Meja sat quietly wondering about what his friend had told him. Life was life to be lived as it came. So he sat and pondered over his friend's words and slowly relaxed. Maina explained to him all about the life in the city, its laws and bye-laws, its corruption, and, whenever he came across any, its good points. He told Meja that in the city everybody minded his own business and none noticed the other. Not as a fellow human being anyway. Everybody had his part to play in the game of life and everybody did just that.

The two waited by the ditch behind the supermarket for the city rubbish collectors to come round. Until then they could not sleep without the risk of ending up in the rubbish dump five miles out of the city. Whenever a night watchman or a policeman was sighted they dived into the spacious culvert to avoid having to explain that somebody had not cleaned their house yet and so they could not go home. Time passed swiftly and the dim backstreet lights came on. The night chill started settling in and conversation was discouraged by the chattering of teeth. And at about ten o'clock the cleaners came and cleaned house. The two boys crept out of their hole and watched as the huge truck rumbled down the road emptying more dustbins. Then when the vehicle had gone and there was no policeman in sight they sprinted across the road and hopped into the largest of the supermarket dustbins. They snuggled close to each other for warmth and immediately fell asleep intoxicated by the foul smell of rotten vegetables.

Meja never went into offices again to look for work. He followed Maina's example and tried to forget that he ever went to school and wanted a job. The thought of his family back home haunted him for a few weeks though – of his parents expecting to hear the good news that he had a job, not knowing that that was exactly the bit of news that they were least likely ever to hear. Yet even had he the courage to go back and tell them the truth, there was the problem of bus fare. So he tucked the memories of his family into the darkest corner of his mind, put on a resigned smile and followed his friend faithfully wherever he went.

Maina taught him a lot of things. He taught him how to look after himself and how to avoid getting involved in other people's business, least of all policemen's. When a policeman was on the beat he did not like to be interfered with, not even if that beat happened to trespass on your sleeping bin. The boys fetched food from bins, slept in bins and lived in the backyards, in bins.

The hot season came, heralded by swarms of flies and a dry dust-carrying wind that swept down the backstreets choking everything. The two young men became dehydrated and their bodies were covered in scales. Food from the bins dwindled and the competition with mongrels increased. The stench of the gutters became almost unbearable and the office messengers no longer dared take their usual short cuts from back door to back door to deliver their never-ending messages. The backstreets were left to the boys and the beggars. Strangely enough, with the increase in the dust, heat and flies there was also an increase in the backstreet population, for some of Maina's old friends fresh from prison and determined to make a fresh start, came back to the old backyards. Maina taught Meja to keep away from them. Once a person tasted the prison life he could not help going there a second time, Maina said.

It was during this season when the human and fly population were rising that Maina started having brainwaves. With the increase in competition this was inevitable. He conferred with his companion and they agreed to have a go at the suburbs of the city. There they tried to get jobs. Usually it was chopping wood or watering cabbages and flowers under the close scrutiny of a storky housewife. The few coins they collected allowed for a little luxury – tea in a cheap roadside kiosk and occasionally Maina had a whole cigarette to himself, one that no one had stepped on. Such a cigarette he would smoke for two days.

The hot season went and the wet season came. The indifferent skies poured their share of misery into the backstreets. The ditches were now urine and rain-swept and no culvert was safe to be lived in. The streets were covered by puddles and the chilly winds pursued the youths into the best sheltered corners of the buildings and lanes. The food from the back of the supermarket was soggy and uneatable long before the two came round to it. Now that the wood-chopping season proper

9

had come, everybody with two hands who could wield an axe invaded the suburbs where the wealthy lived. Competing against the rest of the world, the boys had no chance. So they turned to other things. Old and battered aluminium utensils, copper wiring, bottles, cans and general scrap metal were to be found in plenty in the rubbish bins. They collected these and sold them to some person who had the privilege of reaching the big dealers. Everything of any economic value went via the middle man to enormous scrap metal dumps in the outskirts of the city. From there only the devil could tell where it next landed.

During this big business season the boys learned one thing. Whatever you did, no matter how you did it, nothing ever paid. Everybody tried to cheat you, from the ragged scrap metal buyer to the barrel woman for whom you chopped wood.

'That's enough,' the woman would say and disappear back into the interior of the house where one dared not follow to complain. Then just at this point the husband would arrive from work and one had to get away before he was noticed.

The metal buyer and his dirty little coins were even worse. He did not talk things over. He dictated.

'Twenty cents,' he said.

'Twenty cents?' Maina complained. 'Why, this bottle alone is worth sixty cents. There is at least two pounds of scrap metal here. Is that all worth twenty cents?'

The scrap king looked the two young men up and down. He feigned annoyance.

'I know about all the prices well,' he said. 'Right now there are too many bottles of this type around. So you see, no market.'

Maina wondered. It had taken him and his partner two weeks to collect ten of the type. And there were too many around!

'Why don't you go around collecting the excess yourself instead of coming to beg for them from us?' he asked the buyer.

'Now you are wasting my time,' the scrap man said. 'Are you selling or not? I am a busy man.' He made as though to lift his sack to his back and go.

Meja was thinking fast. Twenty cents per bottle added up to two shillings the lot. The scrap metal was about one shillings worth. Three shillings were better than a lot of old bottles you could not eat. Maina was of the opinion of smashing up all the bottles and saying the hell with scrap metal dealers.

'Wait,' Meja said to the busy man. 'Make it twenty-five cents each.'

'Twenty cents,' the old man swung the sack onto his back.

'Cheat,' Maina called him.

They ended up selling their goods at the buyer's price. The old man hobbled away feeling satisfied and the boys sat back away from the drizzle watching him go and trying to make some sort of a budget.

Meja looked at the coins in his hands. They were all old and battered and the hole in the middle of each ten cents piece told of nothing but emptiness and deficiency. Scraps of coins for scraps of metal. What a deal!

He shook his head. If only he could reach the big dealer, the source of the money. But he was so high up there somewhere and they right at the bottom rung of the ladder which only the cheating ragged man knew how to ascend.

'If only I could reach the main scrap buyers,' he told his partner, 'if only I could, I would collect all the metal dustbins in this street and pawn them for real money.'

Maina smiled a weary smile.

'And then where would we sleep?' he asked.

Meja scratched his head thoughtfully.

'I think I would leave one,' he said.

'No need,' Maina said and patted him on the back. 'We would both be deep in prison long before we had a chance to spend the money.'

They laughed nervously.

The drizzle increased to a steady downpour which by the time it stopped would leave all the culverts and bins flooded beyond habitation.

2

THE OLD MAN hobbled down the backstreet with his large myopic eyes darting this way and that. Every now and then he stopped to look uncomfortably behind him or to peer into one of the large wastebins that littered the pavement. The stink was overwhelming and his large negroid nose twitched uncontrollably. The afternoon sun was hot and under his white starched suit the old man felt very uncomfortable. His sandals were dust-covered and slippery from sweat. Through the straps of the sandals the horny toes peeped timidly out.

He came to the end of the street and stopped. He thrust his hand into the pocket of his jacket and fished out a ragged handkerchief. He mopped his face and neck and then passed the rag over his sparsely haired head. All the time his large red eyes scanned the area. A few people passed by and in their hurry to get out of the mucky zones failed to notice him. But neither did the old man pay any attention to them. He just peered into the shadowy street and mumbled to himself incessantly. Then he turned left and trudged along the alley that passed behind the back of the supermarket. On his right was the unused parking lot and on the left the back walls of the shops, high and defiant.

'They should be somewhere here,' he thought as he went. 'I know they are somewhere here,' and he looked at his old pocket watch. It was getting late. He had to get the boys and move fast or he would be late in preparing dinner. And his master never accepted any excuse for meals being late. The old man quickened his pace, all the time looking this way and that.

Directly behind the supermarket he found them. The two young men were dressed in rags and their dirty black bodies showed through the rents in their rags. In front of them on dirty old newspapers were the customary variety of fruits in various stages of rot. The boys were eating and talking in low tones and did not notice the old man as he edged closer. Then the old man coughed timidly and the two sprang up. They eyed the old man suspiciously, their scanty muscles tense. The old man was curious and frightened at the same time. The two youths eyed him like two wild cats and his negroid nose quivered with fear.

'Eh, don't be afraid,' he said fearfully, 'I will not hurt you.'

The boys looked at one another and one of them spoke.

'We are not afraid,' he said. 'And you cannot hurt us.'

The old man shifted his feet restlessly. His fear told him to get the hell out of the backstreets and away from the fierce boys. But his master needed two youths, two cheap youths to work for him. If there were any cheap youths anywhere, here they were.

'I want to help you,' he told them.

The two looked at one another again and the one who had spoken laughed.

'Did you hear that, Meja?' he told his companion. 'The old crow wants to help us.'

Meja laughed too, but a little less heartily.

He studied the old man again, from the red pig-tailed cap down the white starched uniform to the shabby sandals. The old man was sweating badly and his thin body trembled under his clothes. His long drooping moustache gave him the appearance of a famished gutter rat.

'We did not ask for help,' Meja's companion told him. 'We can take care of ourselves.'

The old man looked furtively this way and that. He edged closer. The boys stepped back and looked around too, their fear of policemen aroused.

'Look boys,' the old man said urgently. 'I like you and . . .'

'We do not like you,' Meja's friend told him.

'Let him speak, Maina,' Meja said. 'Let us hear how he came to like us.' He turned to the trembling old man. 'Who are you and what do you want?'

The old man licked his dry lips and grinned a hideous toothless grin. Slimy brown tobacco spittle seeped down the corners of his mouth. Maina grimaced.

'I am Boi,' the old man said. 'My . . .'

'Boy!' Maina exclaimed. 'Have you lost your way to the asylum old man? You must have made a wrong turning. We cannot direct you though. We have not been there, yet.'

The old man trembled openly. He took out his rag of a handkerchief and dried off the sweat which flowed down his face and neck.

'What do you want, Boi?' Meja asked him.

Maina moved to interrupt but Meja stopped him with his raised hand.

'Well?' he encouraged the old man.

He felt the old man had something important on his mind, to make him brave the notorious backstreets.

'My master,' the old man stammered. 'My master wants two boys . . .'

'What you mongrel?' Maina shouted and moved towards the old man menacingly.

He had heard of some masters who sent their workers into the

13

backstreets to bring them boys to satisfy their sexual needs. It had sounded a great joke then.

Meja did not understand what it was all about.

'What did you say?' he asked stepping between the two. 'What does he want?'

'Boys,' Boi said. 'Boys to work for him in his gardens. He will pay you well and he is not a bad white man.'

'Go tell him to . . .' Maina began to say.

'What is the pay?' Meja enquired.

Boi cleared his throat and shook his head. He was regaining self-confidence.

'I don't know but I am sure it is good pay,' he said. 'Food, accommodation and . . .'

'Accommodation?' Maina said. 'Go tell him to accommodate his grandmother.'

'Where is your master?' Meja asked ignoring his partner.

Boi glanced at the threatening Maina and back to Meja.

'He lives in a farm twenty miles from the city,' he said. 'He is in town for shopping and will take you to the farm with him if you want to work for him.'

Meja turned to Maina. 'What do you say?' he asked him.

Maina's face twisted as he picked a rotten orange from the remains of their interrupted dinner and handed it to Meja.

'Give him this to take to his rotten master,' he said.

Meja's face was tense with anxiety. He looked at the hand holding the orange and then at the face. He did not understand what had got into his friend.

'You don't want the job?' he asked.

'Not that sort of job, sorry,' Maina shook his head. 'Not me, never.'

Meja was surprised.

'A few months back you were ready to take on anything,' he said to Maina. 'So was I and still am. If you will not work in the garden for money, I will. If you choose to remain in this stinking place, I don't.'

Maina folded his fist tight.

'You don't know what you are talking about,' he told Meja. 'His master wants a wife not a gardener.'

Meja looked back at Boi in confusion, then slowly but surely realisation dawned. He too was now shocked and disgusted.

'What is he talking about?' Boi asked full of concern.

'Your master,' Meja told him. 'Is he . . . has he got a wife?'

'He has a wife and four children,' Boi told him. 'But don't worry. His gardens need care and he will pay you well. He will let you alone to do your work and then pay you well.'

Maina deflated like a balloon. He looked away from Meja's smiling face.

'See now,' Meja told him. 'Your evil mind is always visualising dirty things.'

Maina threw the rotten orange to the ground.

'Tell your master to go to . . .' he began to say.

'You don't want the job?' Meja asked him again.

Maina shook his head.

'An earthworm, not me,' he announced.

Meja looked from his friend to the dirty backstreet and the waste-bins. Though he had not done so since first he arrived from the village, he could smell again the horrible stink that filled the air. His nose twisted involuntarily. It was incredible that anyone would choose to remain here rather than work on a farm where food and accommodation were provided free of charge. He looked back at the clean old man.

'I will do anything to get out of here,' he said to himself. 'Let us go,' he told Boi.

Although Maina was dead against going to work in any garden any-where, Meja was in for anything that might spell money. But what he wanted most of all was to get out of the back alleyways and taste human food again and sleep under a roof out of the rain and the wind and cold. If Boi's master had promised only food and accommodation, he might still have agreed to go work for him.

Of course Maina was not one to be left alone in the wilderness. They had lived together for too long to part just like that. If rain and storms and scrap-iron buyers had failed to separate them a little mad man known as Boi would not succeed.

Boi could not have struck a better bargain. What his master had asked for was a cheap gardener, not a professional gardener. The two youths he had adopted would do the work all right. And Boi would get credit from his master for finding them, though that was all he could hope for, since the very mention of a rise in pay could cause a riot in the house. Boi had learned this and did not complain. That was how he had managed to keep his job as a cook during the past forty years.

The big master (he weighed 250 pounds) and his family did not care who worked in their garden. All they cared was that someone should do so, do it well, and for as little as possible.

But Boi had told the boys that the white man would leave them alone to do their jobs. That was a lie. There was a foreman who represented the white boss and to him no work was well done enough.

The farm was bigger than the two new hands had suspected. It was on a plain, flat and windy and most of the time dry. The farmhouse was surrounded by tall cedar trees that protected it from wind, and nearby an old fashioned windmill pumped water from a stream into a reservoir perched on tall posts behind the house.

A respectable distance from the farmhouse and its always creaking windmill was the farmhands' village. The huts were crowded together to save land for the more important wheat and maize fields. The huts sat back, some leaning to one side, in a sad group as subdued and resigned as the occupants who day by day toiled on the farm for their miserable pay. All round the camp chicken runs, dog kennels and vegetable gardens fought for space. From early morning when the sun rose and there was a little hope for the future, dust, chickens, mongrels and children played together and waited for the sun to go down and mother to come back from her work in the faraway fields, and prepare the only meal for the day.

It was in this village, where life made no boundaries between little children and puppies, that Maina and Meja were to live. They were given a hut each, but they were used to living so close together in the dustbins that neither could stand the loneliness of a whole hut to himself, and they decided to move into one of the huts and leave the other vacant. The great problem then was which one to move into. They inspected each hut in turn carefully, then sat down to debate which of the two was the more liveable. Both leaned to one side, and the thatch of each was old, mice infested and leaking. Now they came to the details that mattered.

Meja's hut was flea-land, and the whole circular wall practically plastered with bed bugs. The floor lay as when it was first created with the rest of the world, rough, corrugated and at least a foot deep in fine dust. Evil black soot hung from the roof like giant stalactites, so heavy that the thatching was caving in. It seemed the builder had been unable to make up his mind which of the two openings to make the door and which one the window, for the window was much wider and taller than the door and about a foot off the ground.

Maina's hut was a little better in a few respects. It was relatively round, less sooty, and, mysteriously, absolutely flea-free. Mice and bed bugs there were, but these were less famished and consequently less hostile according to Maina's reasoning. Thus Maina's hut was voted the most habitable.

Boi told them a few things before he scuttled off in the direction of the farmhouse and his duties. They were to be provided with a tinful of maize meal every evening at six o'clock, and that only if the foreman was satisfied by the day's work. They were also to get a pint of skimmed milk. They were to report every morning at six o'clock at the food store to be issued with duties for the day, and later in the

16

evening for the ration. Boi's hut was a few huts away and they could go to him if they wanted any assistance. Nothing was said during this lecture about cooking utensils or bedding for the new farm workers.

Later in the evening the two turned up at the store for their ration. They fell into the long queue with the rest of the population and proceeded slowly to the door of the store where the storky foreman stood between a sack of flour and a drum of paper-white watery milk that had just been skimmed and was still warm from the machine. Meja was in front of Maina and he fell under the foreman's scrutiny.

'You are the new boys?' the foreman asked.

'Yes.'

'From the city?'

'Yes.'

'What work were you doing there?'

Meja hesitated. Maina helped out. 'Nothing,' he said.

The foreman looked from one to the other and back. He did not hide his contempt for the idle city idiots.

'What work did your old man do?' he went on. 'He ought to have taken you to school. Or maybe he did and you ran away from school. Is that what you did?'

Meja shifted his feet uncomfortably. He looked up at the huge foreman. Big belly, massive hands, rounded fat cheeks and mean little eyes. It took men like him to make the others miserable.

Maina spoke up.

'Our old men do not live in the city,' he said. 'They took us to school and we did not run away.'

'One of them boys, huh?' the foreman breathed. 'You city boys are known for your arrogance. Here you had better look out.'

Someone in the queue behind grumbled. Another complained loudly. The queue was being held up for too long. The foreman glanced in the direction of the complainant and took his time about it. Then he slowly refilled the measuring tin and stretched it to Meja.

'If anybody gets tired of waiting he is allowed to go away,' he said.

Then he noticed Meja standing confused looking at the tinful of flour.

'Where is your bag?' he asked.

'We have no bags,' Maina said.

The foreman looked from one to the other and he was curious this time.

'Bottles?'

'We don't have anything,' Maina told him. 'Not even cooking utensils.'

'Where is your stuff?'

'We have none.'

'What were you using in the city for cooking?'

'We did not cook.'

'And what the hell did you eat?' the foreman was getting irritated. 'Oh, I remember. You city people are famous for your love of hotel food. Too bad we have no hotels here. You will have to learn to cook for yourselves. Better get something to put your stuff in before I close the store.'

The two fell out of queue and went hunting for containers. Then in the midst of their desperation they remembered Boi and his offer of help. And Boi was kind enough to sell them two tin mugs, two tin plates, two aluminium cooking pots, and two old blankets and a collection of sacks to sleep on. That night in their own hut they had their first self-served meal ever. It took them most of the evening to prepare and it was certainly better than the fruit from the back of the market.

Boi came over for a chat that night and told them more about farm life. He had taken them over as his two adopted sons and made no effort to hide the fact that they would be required to honour him. If they followed his sound advice they would do well. If they didn't, anything could happen.

The two made their beds by the flickering firelight when their saviour had gone. Then they prepared to go to bed.

'This place strikes me as funny,' Maina said. 'First there is a foreman who is all power and knowledge; and a lot of people he leads around like sheep. Then there is an old cook who is over-eager to help in exchange for some money that has not been earned yet. You know, very unlike life in the city where everybody is big in his own way and minds his own business.' He looked round the warm dimly lit hut. 'I like it much better here though. Very unlike the back of the supermarket.'

Meja said nothing. They got each into his bed.

'You know what, Meja?' Maina said seriously. 'I am not sure I am going to like the foreman.'

'You have not given him any reason to like you either,' Meja told him and turned on to his side.

During the first few months of work on the farm, Meja and Maina did almost all the jobs there were, in the effort to find one to suit them. Strangely enough it never occurred to anyone to separate them: since they were sharing one grown up man's pay it seemed they might as well do the same job. They started with looking after cattle, killed three rodents in the course of one week and were duly disqualified from cattle handling – one could not mix cattle herding and rodent-hunting and do well at either. The farm machinery and the extensive wheat fields that stretched on either side of the farmhouse as far as the

18

eye could see were both out of their reach. So the two eventually landed in the styes cleaning and feeding the pigs. That season for the first time in many years, the farmer lost the best-boar trophy at the agricultural show, the pig-feeding supervisor was fired and the boys found themselves ejected from pig handling. They landed in the orchards next. Like in every other job on the farm there was an orchard boss, an older wrinkled farmhand who believed that orchards and city oafs could not rhyme.

Meja and his companion could not remember when they had last seen whole ripe oranges. They made use of the slight pause in their travel through jobs and ate oranges. There were other types of fruit in the gardens but these were of no particular interest. The boys ate themselves sick of oranges and then ate some more. Inevitably the orchard boss had them whisked from the fruit and dumped into the farmhouse gardens. There, there were no oranges but flower beds and a small garden that provided vegetables for the master's kitchen.

Working at the farmhouse placed them at a disadvantage. As well as being under the direct rule of their big master, who was even harder to please than the foreman, they fell under the scanning radar of Boi that missed nothing. It seemed Boi could see anyone idling in the garden through the wall of the kitchen, and without having to look up from his culinary duties.

The two boys worked under the supervision of everybody and Boi. And the Boi they had met from the backstreets was different from the Boi they now worked under. The Boi of the backstreets had been tired-looking, frightened and eager to please. The Boi they had at the farm was fatherly, in a bossy way, self-assured, and shouted unnecessary orders all the time. Nothing to him was ever perfectly done. And when Boi was not shoving them about, the boss was around doing it person-ally. And his means were severe. Nobody was to stop and rest or worse to sit and rest. He and the foreman exacted punishment if any of the workers was found idling. Thus it happened that one afternoon, one of those afternoons that one cannot help dozing off, Meja was found by the boss lying asleep by the stream. Without any ceremony, the big man lifted the youth and kicked him right into the middle of the stream. Gasping and struggling for breath, Meja surfaced and held on to the water-weeds at the edge of the stream. All the time he shouted insults at the idiot who had dared to kick him when he was not even looking. Then he cleared the water from his eyes and his words choked him. What he had expected was a big brawny youth or a frail old man, not the giant who now stood at the edge of the stream. His master's clothes were bulging with the rolls of fat that lay behind them, and his puffy cheeks were soft and curled into a funny contented smile.

'So I am a stinking idiot, am I?' the master's voice boomed.

'No . . . no . . . sir,' Meja whispered. 'I did not know it was you.'

'And how dare you sleep when you know that I am paying you to work,' the master roared, his little smile fading.

'I was not sleeping,' Meja complained. 'I was only . . .'

'You were only innocently counting the number of pails of water you were to take to the house, weren't you?' the master said.

That was exactly what Meja had been doing before he fell asleep. He did not tell his master this though. Already his rosy face was deformed by the funny little smile again.

'I know what is wrong with you,' Meja's master went on, 'they are giving you too much to eat. I will see Boi about that. My farm is not a home for juvenile delinquents.'

Meja was enraged by being called a juvenile delinquent, and he had the impulse to tell his master who he thought was having too much to eat. But seeing the ham hands and the massive belly, he decided against it. Those hands could cause a lot of damage if let loose on a youngster like himself.

'Don't sit there staring at me like an overgrown toad,' his master roared on. 'Get that pail to the gardens.' Then he added as an after-thought: 'Full of water.'

Then he lumbered up the path breathlessly and headed for the farm-house.

Slowly, Meja picked himself from the mud and collected the bucket from the bank. Filling it, he laboured painfully up the slight slope to the house. Halfway there he met Maina. Maina had been recently promoted to helping in the kitchen because he was 'better behaved' than Meja. As far as Meja could figure out, Maina had never done anything worthy of any praise around the farm. He had, though, acquired an uncanny way of getting all his pilfering pinned on someone else – Meja.

'What is new in the garden?' Maina asked Meja.

'A lot of weed and you can go steal it if you like,' Meja told him 'What is cooking in the kitchen?'

'A lot of trouble,' Maina told him. 'The cook is raving about some cakes he had left on the table that have now disappeared. I was there all the time and I never saw them disappear. I tell you, Meja, I did not see them.'

Meja scrutinised Maina's pockets. They were bulging.

'You can't pin this one on me, Maina,' Meja told him. 'And if you don't want your ration slashed you will take those cakes back.'

'I did not . . .' Maina started to say, then caught Meja's eyes on his pockets. 'All right Meja,' he said changing the tone. 'I was bringing them to you but if you say so, I will take them back.'

'If you want to know, I am already at half ration for stopping at the

20

stream to think,' Meja told him. 'I was hoping you would not be put on the same thing too or we'll starve. Take them back.'

Maina nodded dumbly.

'I will take them back,' he said and went racing up the path.

Some way up the path he stopped. He came back.

'How shall I say they reappeared,' he asked.

Meja wanted to tell him that was his headache and then remembered Maina's wicked way of getting things pinned on him.

'Just put them back,' he advised. 'Say the same as before if you like. You did not see them reappear.'

Maina turned to go and his friend noticed a wicked smile playing at his lips.

'Look, Maina,' Meja told him. 'Don't try to tell the cook that you had to take them back from me. I was right in the middle of the stream at the precise minute you stole the cakes. The fat pig will testify that. He kicked me in.'

Maina looked at his friend's clothes, noticing for the first time that they were wet and muddy.

'So the boss caught you dodging work as you always do, did he?' he said raising his eyebrows. 'I knew he would.'

He went up to the house laughing loudly.

Meja watched him go and shook his head. Maina and his impish ways annoyed and fascinated him at the same time. All he thought of was food and fun. Heartaches and disappointments were strangers to him. Here they were, two educated young men earning one-tenth of what their education entitled them to and living under forced labour conditions, and yet Maina had time for mischief. Their education and the backstreet were to Maina as remote as his family was now. Occasionally, as befits any normal being, he became moody, but that was only occasionally. It took important issues to make Maina sad, like when the foreman had been over-careless with the measuring tin and had only blown flour dust into Maina's container. On one of these occasions Maina said to Meja:

'If the foreman's arm does not improve I will have to call his attention to its shaky condition. I would like to have full measure once in a while too.'

Meja sometimes remembered his family. At times he did so with bitter regret and longing and at times with amused detachment. He wanted to write or go back and see his people, but he did not know what to say in the letter. The prospects of facing his family after the backstreet life were not very bright either. They were still waiting to hear from him, he felt, but he could never dream of accumulating the necessary money to satisfy their needs. Not at the rate at which it was coming in.

The sixty shillings they were paid each month was hardly enough to exist on. But by scaling his needs almost to the level of starvation he did manage to save at least one pound every month. His family would need at least twenty times that amount for their daily needs each month. That to Meja meant that they were living at minus twenty pounds every month. He did not want to think of this so he let himself be carried away by the other's carelessness. They rarely talked about their homes and family, all they thought of was food and a place to lay their heads when night came. And the world was dark, cold, lonely and miserable.

Meja was on his way from the stream for the third time when he found his friend waiting for him all shaken.

'Meja, it is no use,' he cried helplessly.

'What is no use?' Meja asked. 'Boi would not believe you and you had to lie about me?'

'Worse than that,' Maina said, 'he believed you might have stolen them all right. Then he raved about their being dirty and said something about making fresh ones for the house and keeping the soiled ones for himself. It was the thought of that old frog feasting on the delicious little cakes that gave me courage. I stole back the cakes, Meja.'

Meja put down the bucket and sighed resignedly: 'Now you have spoilt it,' he said shrugging.

Then he thought for a moment. He was also dead against letting Boi defile the little cakes. And he was already on half-ration so it did not matter. He had nothing to lose.

'Where are the cakes?' he asked.

'They are here,' Maina said almost too eagerly.

They sat down right there by the path and started eating, all caution gone out of them. Meja knew he would be held responsible for the theft after all. Maina would make sure that he was. He would be the prosecution witness. Then the usual half tin of flour and half all would follow.

'You know, Meja,' Maina said his mouth full of cake. 'I had buried these cakes in the garden when the cook was first looking for them.'

'Well, was that supposed to be proof of my guilt?' Meja asked.

Maina sniggered.

'Don't be angry, Meja,' he told him. 'That will not make any difference. Boi will never learn to like you. He tells me this often. And you are still an earthworm, a manual labourer. They could not take you to a worse job in this farm. They could take you to swine feeding again, but then you would starve the bastards again.' He shrugged. 'You are already on half-ration. If they take me out of the kitchen there will be no more left-over crumbs for us and no decent food any more. So you see, I had to remain blameless.'

22

And now Meja had a feeling he knew why Maina had been promoted to a kitchen-boy. From the beginning, Boi had been afraid of Maina. So to keep him on his side Boi had him promoted to make sure he did not do things behind the cook's back.

It had never crossed Maina's mind that Meja might be promoted to working in the kitchen if ever he was demoted. To him, Meja was destined for hoes and watering cans. His hands and feet and even his strong young shoulders were shaped for bending over little young shoots and tending them. And what did Meja know about working in the kitchen anyway? Had he not failed to get a job as a kitchen boy in the cheap Arab restaurant only a few months back? Brains is what it took to work in a kitchen, especially a farmhouse kitchen, and he, Maina, told his friend this many times. So as far as Maina was concerned, Meja had to work in the garden and like it or go back to the backstreets. The choice was his to make.

'What are you sad about?' the kitchen-boy asked the earthworm.

'I am not sad,' Meja answered. 'I was just wondering how many cakes there were originally. Were there only eight?'

'No, there were ten,' Maina answered innocently. 'But surely I was not going to take those cakes back for nothing, was I? The cook had to give me something for recovering them.'

'You mean . . .' Meja began to protest.

'What is so bad about it?' Maina interrupted. 'After all I brought the others to share with you.'

Meja said nothing. There was no use arguing with the unscrupulous devil. He would win in the end. But there was one good point about Maina. Whatever he stole from the kitchen he always brought to share with his friend. The only thing they never shared was blame. Maina liked Meja so much he let him keep the whole blame for himself.

'About the halved ration,' Meja said. 'A twelve-ounce pound of flour and a few grams milk is the grand ration. I try to halve that to get our new diet, but I get decimals and you cannot eat decimals.'

'The answer is easy,' Maina said beaming with pleasure. 'Starvation is the answer. But I am not concerned with that right now. After all there is your garden of carrots we can always turn to.'

'That is another trouble,' Meja told him. 'Boi has cooked all of them.'

Maina showed real concern.

'You mean there is nothing we can eat?' he asked.

Meja shook his head.

'Only weed,' he answered. 'But there is not a single carrot.'

'Carrots, boys,' a voice boomed behind them.

They shot to their feet at the unmistakable sound.

'Conspiring to steal my carrots at night is punishable by dismissal,' he rumbled.

'We . . .' Meja started to say, but the accusing look on Maina's face stopped him.

Their employer missed this though.

'As I was saying,' he went on, 'the foreman is giving you too much to eat. You are both on half-ration already. You are going on half-pay as well.' He laughed, exposing rows of white teeth and a red mouth. The rolls of blubber round his neck danced vigorously like rings of necklaces.

The two young men did not argue with him. They knew that one word was enough to send them back to the backstreets express. He left them standing side by side, two underfed young men.

'Half ration, – starvation,' Maina said to himself. 'Half pay, – misery and insanity and . . .'

He did not finish. Boi called and he marched back to the kitchen to explain the redisappearance of the cakes.

Meja watched him go, wondering. Whoever said that misfortunes did not come singly knew what he was talking about. But why the devil should have materialised just when such a notion was on the carpet he did not understand. Luckily though the cakes had just vanished or the boss might have asked by whose permission cakes were grown in his flower gardens. That big boy could phrase questions.

Meja spat on to the palms of his rough hands in readiness for the bucket. Just then, he saw Maina racing down the path with Boi, a broom-stick in hand, hobbling after him. This was evidence that Boi did not believe whatever explanation Maina had offered for the re-disappearance of the cakes. Too bad for him.

Shrugging, Meja picked up his bucketful of water and headed for the flower beds. Theirs was a domestic quarrel and he knew how to mind his own business. His fight was in the garden, with the weeds.

3

MEJA SCRAPED the last bits of food from his dish and shovelled them into his mouth. Maina was busy licking his plate and then his fingers. He did it slowly and methodically. He started with the little finger of his right hand and worked towards the thumb. Meja stopped for a moment to watch him. The fire burned low and the small tin lamp threw grotesque shadows on the walls of the little hut.

The only furniture in the room were the two packing crates they sat on, and a camping type rack in one corner, on which they kept their meagre utensils (two tin mugs, two tin plates, a huge can and two aluminium cooking pots). On one side of the hut was Meja's bed, and Maina's on the other, each a collection of sacks and rags thrown on the flea-ridden earth floor. The fire was built between three large stones in the middle.

'That is what I call a good meal,' Maina said.

He sent the tin plate flying on to the rack to await washing the following morning.

Meja placed his plate close to the fire and sent forth a healthy belch.

'I agree with you,' he said. 'But for a little too much salt, the vegetables were good. The flour could have done with a little more cooking too.'

'What do you know about cooking,' Maina growled. 'Is food the swirl you prepare when I let you? You know very well even the Fat Pig's dogs would not eat the leftovers if there were any.'

'Talking of the Fat Pig,' Meja said. 'What were you debating with his son when I saw you talking so earnestly?'

'I was trying to convince him that I have been to school,' Maina said. 'You see, he found me singing to myself, so we got talking. He did not believe that I had done the bloody exam. He said I ought to be working in the city like himself. You see, he did his examination last year but one, like you, and he has been working ever since. So he wanted to know what I was doing working in a farm. I told him I love working in the kitchen and he believed me.'

Meja laughed.

'Who would not?' he said. 'You act like you never liked any other job in the world better. Did you tell him I love tending flowers too?'

B   25

'You don't act like you enjoy it,' Maina told him. 'No wonder you are always on half something or other.'

'You know, I have been thinking,' Meja said. 'I am getting tired of being thrown about by everybody. One minute, half-ration, the next half-pay. It is getting so that I cannot stand it any longer. If one is working he must also eat. If this goes on, I will . . .'

Maina burst out laughing. Meja watched him curiously.

'What is funny about what I am saying,' he enquired.

'It is funny to think you could go back to the backstreets, voluntarily,' Maina said through laughter.

'And what about going to the front streets for a change?' Meja asked.

'You?' Maina said. 'With your speed you would not last an hour. Out there it needs a person who is all speed and cunning. Brains are an essential part of the game too, and right in the middle of the chest, a large, large heart. You must be able to stand the sorts of treatment they hand out to you once caught.'

Meja's face lit up.

'Should I take it then,' he said, 'that you are slow, stupid, without any brains at all and with only a pea of a heart in your chest?'

Maina quickly looked up.

'What do you mean?' he grunted.

'You have never been to the main streets, have you?' Meja asked full of smiles for a chance to revenge.

Maina realised his mistake.

'I was there once,' he said solemnly. 'I was looking for a job. They threw me back into the backstreets and I had not the courage to go back and have another try.'

'So you . . .' Meja began.

'Let us not talk about that,' Maina told him seriously.

Meja started to laugh foolishly then stopped. Maina had just fallen into one of his rare gloomy moods. And when Maina was in one of these instant depressions he talked little of his past life. He just sat, stared at nothing and said nothing. Sometimes he would go away into the bush all alone and sit down and cry. He would sit there toying with his dreams and his fears and his memories and he would cry softly to himself. Then feeling renewed, he would dry his tears, put on a smiling mask and walk briskly back to reality as merry as ever, and no one would know anything had happened.

Meja watched him quietly, now and then throwing a few more twigs into the fire.

'I am sorry, Maina,' he said, although he did not know why he was sorry. But he did not want to see Maina in that condition. He liked

26

Maina smiling and telling dirty jokes about his boss, Boi, and the pig of a foreman.

Maina said nothing. He stared at the wall of the hut, his lips drawn tight and his eyes hard and expressionless. Outside a light rain was falling and night insects cried for mercy. Through the cracks on the door of the hut a cold draught of air swept into the room and the flame of the tin lamp flickered incessantly.

'Are you angry at me?' Meja ventured although he knew the answer.

'No,' Maina said.

'What then?'

Maina sighed.

'I was just thinking,' he said. 'Eating from waste bins, sleeping in them and hanging around the backstreets, as though we have no homes. And nobody seems to understand or care,' he stopped talking and for a moment stared at his friend. 'What did I tell you the first time you met me in the backstreet well dressed and hungry? What did I tell you, Meja?'

'That there was no job anywhere?' Meja said.

'No, about going back home,' Maina told him.

'That you are no earthworm?' Meja asked.

'Yes, that was what I told you,' Maina said, going back to staring at the dimly lit wall of the hut. 'But that was not the reason. I was lying to disguise the truth. The truth is I am afraid, I cannot go back home because there is no place to go back home to. My father owns two acres of land. Not big enough for even one little hut. So he has bought a house in the village and uses the land for food. I have three brothers and two sisters at home. The bit of land is not enough.'

He stopped and sighed. Meja watched and fingered his once smooth chin which now had a crop of sprouting black hair.

'When I was sent to school, it was in the hope that one day I would get a good job and become independent,' Maina went on. 'My father made no secret of this. He told me, Meja. He did and was serious about it. I took my share of his wealth with my education. He told me this too. You see why I can't go back there? It would be cheating if I went back because the others did not go to school. It is not my fault though; I did my best at school. Did I tell you about being a book-worm?'

Meja nodded and grunted. His mouth was dry and he could not speak. As Maina spoke he listened and drew parallels with his own sad story.

'So when I tell you that I cannot go back, Meja, it is not because I fear work,' Maina went on. 'They would not want me back there even though they might not say it. I would only increase their misery. I would only go back if I got a job. Then I would buy a blanket for my

27

father, an overcoat for my mother and go back to tell them I am still alive. Believe me or not, until I get a job, I may as well be dead. It is no use being alive if I cannot help them. I know this because my father told me. You might think he is cruel, but knowing the conditions at home, you would think otherwise. My father was very wise. And maybe one day, I will go back home and tell him so.'

Meja added more twigs to the fire and the smoke from the slightly wet twigs made his eyes water.

'Maybe you could go back there soon,' he suggested.

Maina stared at him then shook his head this way and that.

'No,' he said. 'You don't understand.'

'I understand,' Meja told him. 'Money is what you must have to go back there. Between us we could collect enough to allow you to go. I could let you have my pay for this month.'

Maina shook his head.

'Thank you for the offer,' he said, 'but that won't do. You see, if I say I am working they will think I am holding back something from them. If I say I am underpaid they won't believe it. A learned person like me can never be underpaid. Again they will expect me to send them money every end of month. What they want is money and they won't understand any other language. It is hopeless.'

Meja shrugged.

Maina sighed.

'Maybe I could lend you my pay,' he said. 'Maybe you would like to go home and . . .'

'No, thanks,' Meja said. 'I cannot. My case is different though. They would want me to go home money or no money, job or no job. Still I owe them something and can't just walk home. I am too cowardly to try.'

'You won't go back, ever?' Maina asked.

'I don't know,' Meja said. 'I really don't know. I would like to. Maybe I will go back there some day.'

'Meanwhile?'

'I will stay here. I will stay here and pretend I am dead.'

'Nothing better. I am with you.'

The rain outside had increased to a steady downpour. The night insects and the hyrax could hardly be heard. The white man's dogs were barking complainingly.

Maina cocked his ears and listened to the barking dogs. He smiled.

'You know that bitch,' he asked. 'The one that yells so sharply?' Meja smiled knowingly.

'Yes,' he said.

'Which one is she?' Maina asked.

'She is the one that looks like the foreman.'

28

'You are wrong.'

'She looks like Boi, then.'

'Wrong again.'

'Nonsense,' Meja said. 'They all look the same. They are dogs.'

Maina grinned.

'That is where you go wrong,' he told him. 'None of them looks like a dog. Just have a closer look at them one of these days. The bitch that looks like Boi has no teeth. The one that looks like a foreman has thirty-two teeth and a nose that runs all day and all night. What this dog lacks is a sense of smell. In fact it has no senses at all. No wonder the flour is never ladled out equally.'

Maina was back on his home ground. The story ran on and on. Every creature on the farm had a double in human form. There was a pig that looked like the boss. There was a cow that looked like a woman teacher they knew back in school, whose deficiency was in udders. There was also an old bay mule that looked like the scrap metal buyer, its bones rattling when it moved just like the scrap dealer's sack. There was even a hyrax that snored and coughed just like Meja. Though he had never seen it, Maina was convinced the hyrax also looked like Meja, for only a mouth exactly like Meja's could make such a racket. Once or twice Maina had awakened Meja in the middle of the night to listen to the echo of his snoring ringing in the distant forest.

'Stop those stories,' Meja told Maina. 'I have heard them before. You told me last night.'

Maina raised his eyebrows in mock surprise.

'Really? What do you want to hear about then.'

'Nothing,' Meja told him. 'Hand me a mug of milk.'

'That is blasphemy. There isn't a drop of real milk anywhere in this farm. There is some milky water in that can though.'

'All right. Hand me a mug of milky water then.'

'On the other hand, I think it would be better if you went to the stream. The water is clear there.'

Meja gave up. He got up, filled himself a mugful of skimmed milk and came back to the fire. He drank while Maina retold some of the dirtiest jokes currently going round the village. But Meja was not listening. He had heard them many times before. So while Maina enjoyed his narrations Meja thought about his flower gardens. They would be taking in the rain water well.

'Let us go to sleep,' Maina suggested when he was exhausted by his monologue.

He stood up, collected the rest of the utensils and threw them on to the rack to await washing. Then he stretched, yawned and walked to the door of the hut. He opened it and a cold drizzle crept into the

29

room. The tin lamp flickered and went out. Smoke blew into Meja's face and he choked.

'Close that door, you . . .' he coughed.

Maina laughed.

'Immediately I urinate,' he said.

Drops of rain fell on his feet as he stood just inside the door and unbuttoned his trousers. He sent a stream of warm urine out into the night but most of it was blown back on to his feet, and all the time Meja, choked by the smoke, complained. Then he stepped back, closed and fastened the door with the old rusty bolt supported by two rusty nails, picked up one of the crates and wedged it against the door. Then he stepped back, and saluted smartly.

'The door is now closed, bolted and crated,' he reported. 'May I go to sleep now?'

'You can go to bed or to hell, I don't care which,' Meja answered in good humour. 'Just leave that door closed.'

He blew into the fire until flames started dancing up and down. Then he relit the tin lamp and stood up. The tin lamp was now dimmer for it had no oil and the wick was dry and thirsty.

'This tin monster is drinking up oil like water,' he said. 'Someone will have to go and milk that tractor for some more diesel oil tomorrow night.'

'There is a very keen-eyed watchman out there and I don't like him,' Maina said. 'The other night he nearly caught me at it. I was coaxing the machine to let out some oil when he shot a beam of torch in my direction. He made me swallow a whole mouthful of diesel oil. I thought we had had it then, but luckily he just went away. We may have to do without a lamp soon.'

'They don't leave the combine harvesters guarded when they leave them out in the plains at night do they?' Meja asked.

'That is a very clever idea,' Maina said. 'Why hadn't I thought of it before?'

They busied themselves with preparing their beds in their respective places. They dropped on their beds and covered themselves just as the lamp and the fire flickered and went out simultaneously.

'My God, look at your bastards up there,' Meja said.

He was lying on his back staring at the sooty rafters.

'What, God's bastards?' Maina asked looking up too. 'The stars?'

'Not God's,' Meja told him. 'Your creatures.'

Then Maina noticed them. In the glow from the fireplace their eyes sparkled just like stars. They made a circle just where the roof met with the wall, and apart from their eyes, they were immobile, their dark grey bodies very still. And they were watching the two sleepers.

'Go away you motherless swine,' Maina shouted at them.

The sparkling eyes did not even blink.

'They don't seem to understand,' Meja told him. 'Try their language. Tell them something interesting. Something they would like to hear. Tell them where you left the unwashed plates. I am sure that is what they want to know.'

He started laughing heartily.

Maina stretched out his hand as slowly as possible and reached for the cold lamp.

'I know something they will understand,' he said. 'See how you like that, beggars,' he shouted.

He hurled the heavy lamp at the gleaming eyes. Even as the can left the hand that threw it, the eyes vanished. Soot showered all over the hut and Meja turned over spitting and coughing and rubbing at his eyes. The tin lamp landed on his back. He howled with pain and groping for it sent it hurtling to the laughing Maina. It missed him narrowly and landed on the utensils on the rack. When the racket had subsided Maina spoke from the safety of his blanket.

'Did you hear their leader howl?' he asked and rolled over laughing.

Meja was busy cleaning soot from his eyes. Maina uncovered his head and looked around. The fire glowed dimmer and the door was hardly visible from their beds. The eyes had reappeared on the rafters. Another moment and they rained down on the two occupants of the hut, a charging mass of furry bodies. Maina saw them come.

'Retreat,' he screamed. 'The bastards are attacking.'

He dived under his blanket and closed all openings. Instinctively Meja ducked under his blanket. Then the dark hut was left to the big fat rats to command. They first stormed and looted the rack where the tin lamp lay forlornly among the unwashed plates and pots. When the plates were clean, they raged through the hut gobbling anything that was edible. Then they started looking for a way under the blankets to the horny feet of the sleepers.

Meja twisted and turned in an effort to discourage them, but in effect he left an unguarded opening. One of the beasts charged in. There was a scuffle under the blanket. Meja leaped to his feet and shook the rat free.

'This cannot go on,' he cried. 'The monsters will even eat us while we are asleep.'

Maina did not move. The rats had retreated to the safety of the rafters from where they watched the troubled Meja.

He looked round the very dimly lit hut and quietly sank back on his rags. He covered himself well, strengthened his defence and holding his breath braced himself to meet the attack. The creatures counter-attacked all right, but this time did not go anywhere near Meja. They

31

scurried across the floor, rattled the rack and walked across the glowing coals in the fireplace. Maina feigned snoring.

Then they heard the faint knocking. It was still raining outside and the caller knocked urgently. They both listened and heard Boi's unmistakable whining.

'That is Boi,' Meja said. 'Go open for your kitchen boss,' he told Maina.

'The minister for hunger and financial retardation himself,' Maina said from his blankets. 'Is that you Big Rat?' he asked.

'Yes, I am the one,' Boi answered the muffled sound.

Maina howled with laughter and twisted and turned, completely forgetting the dark furred beasts. Meja joined him in the laughter.

'Let the rats provide him with a guard of honour,' Meja said. 'You are welcome, your highness Big Toad.'

The two youths laughed loudly.

Boi was standing half in the rain and half in the shelter of the eaves. He squeezed closer to the door and waited for it to be opened. Then the drizzle caught up with him and he leaned on the door. He leaned just a little too heavily.

With a complaining screech, the two rusty nails holding the bolt came off. The crate supporting the door tipped over and the door flew open. The rats shot back to the rafters. With an astonished cry, Boi staggered into the room, tripped on the packing crate and catapulted across the room to the fireplace. He sat on the hot ashes dazed and for a moment did not feel the heat.

Two curious heads popped from under two dusty blankets and looked around. A cold wind wafted into the hut and from the very dim light of the night outside they saw him. The old man was sitting where the fireplace ought to have been, groaning. No one moved and even the night momentarily held its breath. Then the old man moved.

He reared to his feet like a titan, his hands rubbing at his bottom, let out an ear-shattering bellow and bolted for the door. He tripped on the packing case once more, and flew through the air to land in the dark, wet, rainy night. He let out another shriek that was lost in the rain as he pelted towards his hut.

Meja sighed.

'He scared the hell out of the guard of honour,' Meja ventured, looking into the night. 'And if you ask me the hairy brutes will never come back to this hut as long as they live.'

Maina laughed.

'Do you think he burned himself badly?' Meja asked.

'Hardly,' Maina said. 'You saw the healthy way he sprinted back to his hut. In any case even if he singed his buttocks, nobody asked him to come in. Or did you?'

Meja said nothing.

'Go to sleep then and stop moaning about the Big Rat,' Maina advised and covered his head.

Another gust of moisty wind blew into the hut.

'Close the door,' Meja told him.

Maina uncovered his head and looked at the open door.

'You don't think he is coming back tonight, do you?' he asked.

'Shut that door,' Meja said impatiently.

Maina got up and walked to the door. He glanced into the night, sniggered and shoved the door shut and felt for the bolt. The bolt was nowhere within reach.

'Whatever did the old man do to the bolt?' he asked.

He supported the door with the fatal crate, and crept back to bed.

'I thought you had bolted the door that last time,' Meja said.

'So did I,' Maina agreed. 'The boy must have grown very strong lately.'

He turned over and made himself more comfortable.

'Say, Meja,' he said suddenly. 'Have you ever wondered where the other half of our halved ration goes? I am sure the white man has nothing to do with it.'

'The minister for economic misplanning and under-development should answer that question himself,' Meja said.

'Maybe he was coming to lecture on that tonight,' Maina suggested. 'Someone ought to tell him we are tired of listening to his silly advice.'

'The old man is very lonely, I suppose,' Meja said. 'He has got to talk to someone. Unfortunately we are the closest.'

'Next time he comes around,' Maina said, 'he will have to pay for my attention. He is so good at selling simple worthless things he ought to know how much he should pay me to listen to his tales.'

'Do you think he has children of his own, a family?' Meja asked.

'I will not be surprised if he is all alone in the world,' the other answered. 'Probably he was too busy cooking for somebody else's wife to think of getting one himself. Such men are queer. They even hate children. Did you know he is the one who discouraged the tots who used to come round for supper every evening?'

'No,' Meja said.

'Yes, he did,' Maina told him, 'and I think I will ask him why one of these days.'

There was a long pause in their conversation. Meja breathed heavily.

'Meja,' Maina called.

'Yes,' the other answered drowsily.

'Meja, do you think we shall ever grow old and have wives and children of our own?' Maina asked.

'I don't know,' Meja told him.

33

'Neither do I,' Maina said.

There was another long pause.

'Meja.'

'What now?' the other spoke sleepily.

'Did you ever have a girl?'

'I had three sisters.'

'Not that. Your girl. A friend.'

'Why?' Meja was wide awake now.

'Well, did you?'

'No,' Meja lied. 'Did you?'

A slight silence followed.

'Yes,' Maina then said and sighed. 'I knew a girl once. Plump little thing. I used to walk around with her and feel good. I wrote her letters at school and we did a lot of good things when we next met. We were very good friends, Meja. I am not sure she would even look at me now. I would not want to see her either.'

He paused for breath.

'Meja, are you listening?' he asked.

'Yes,' the other answered also remembering his childhood romances.

'We dreamed a great lot too, me and this girl,' Maina went on. 'I was to write her as soon as I got a job and make her dreams come true. But all that is wasted labour now. None of these things will ever come true. We . . .'

'Go to sleep,' Meja told him.

'Are you not interested?'

'No.'

Maina sighed.

'You are clever, Meja,' he said. 'It is no good remembering. It only hurts. It hurts a bit.'

They kept quiet for some time listening to the night and the rain beat its rhythm on the thatch. It was all so sentimental.

Maina gave a slight cry, caught a bed bug and crushed it between his finger and thumb. Involuntarily he smelt the finger and groaned.

Meja was becoming drowsy again.

Maina laughed suddenly remembering Boi.

'Did you see the way Boi leapt from the rain on to the hot ash?' he asked.

Meja mumbled something unintelligible and started snoring softly. The snoring increased.

'Stop that noise, damn you,' Maina complained.

Meja continued snoring.

Maina felt for something to throw at him and finding nothing turned over to sleep. A rat moved over the rack and the crockery rattled.

'Can't one get rid of you beggars?' he grumbled. 'I thought the minister had fixed you good and proper.'

The rat chose to ignore him. The rain outside increased and the wind howled. The door rattled badly and almost flew open again. The white man's dogs started baying.

For weeks, Boi glided around rather more stiffly than usual and never sat down outside his house. Even in his house he did not sit down. He lay down on his stomach. After cooking on his feet a whole day, he ate on his feet and was very exhausted when he finally dropped on his stomach on his bed and went to sleep. And he dared not tell anyone of his misfortune. How could he possibly explain to the white man without sounding ridiculous. So he lay on his bed exhausted every evening and planned his revenge. He would have liked to ask the employer to sack the boys, but did not know how to put it without sounding malicious.

The relationship between him and the boys deteriorated. His myopic red eyes did not seem to notice the two of them and he handed out orders as if to automata. When he could, he had their rations halved, but that did not satisfy him. He wanted the boys to apologise, fall in front of him and beg for mercy. He believed they had played a dirty trick on him; so they would have to pay for it dearly.

Strangely enough the young men kept out of the old man's way. Meja lost himself in the weeds and was hardly ever seen except by Maina. Maina did his part of the kitchen work, then got out to chat with Meja, leaning on the posts fencing the large vegetable garden behind the house. They talked about the current affairs of the farmhouse and sometimes discussed Boi.

'The Big Toad seems to have grown very lonely these last weeks,' Meja said.

Maina raised his shoulders.

'He should have known better than to sit on hot ash,' he muttered.

Meja strangled a few weeds which threatened to choke a cabbage shoot and uprooted them.

'Say, Maina,' he said straightening up. 'Why don't you try to ease him up. Tell him we did not mean it and . . .'

'Did not mean what?' Maina interrupted. 'We did not shove him into the fire. He broke into our house without permission and *he* ought to apologise for it. Go and apologise to him yourself for breaking down our door.'

Meja nodded slowly.

'I get your point,' he said, 'but I am just sick of the situation. I am tired of losing myself among the cabbages. I want to go back to joking with him and heckling him just as before. Life was better that way.'

'It was,' Maina consented, 'but we did not change it. He did. Let him remake it or rot. As long as he does not meddle with my affairs, I will let him be.' He turned and marched back to the kitchen to answer Boi's call.

Meja stood knife in hand and watched him go.

'So be it,' he said to himself.

And it was.

Boi stirred trouble. His hunger for revenge grew within him and soon he could contain it no longer. He could no longer hide his rage and he barked orders louder than usual. Often he would make the young men do a piece of work over again. Maina washed the floor of the kitchen until his shoulders ached and Meja watered the vegetable gardens until the shoots were almost throwing up water, before they were granted permission to stop. On two occasions Boi poured water on the clean floor of the kitchen and Maina had to wash and polish it all over again. Boi pretended that this was not intentional, but all the same Maina marked it up for reference. And Boi made Meja water the grass on the lawn which had never been watered since the farmhouse was built.

'Now he is crossing the boundary,' Maina told Meja, 'and if he keeps on at this rate, he will soon provoke me to anger. I will have to take action.'

Meja looked down at his muddy hands; muddy from watering the patch of wasteland.

'What will you do?' he asked. 'Beat him up?'

Maina shook his head.

'Nothing that foolish,' he said. 'We would be sacked for sure. I will beat him at his guerrilla tactics. His own primitive tricks. I will know how to retaliate. Just let him cross further into my territory.'

Boi did not stop his harrassments and Maina had to go into action. The counter-attack was launched one day while Boi was busy inspecting the floor of the kitchen. Maina turned off the electric cooker on which the midday meal for the family was cooking, then he busied himself with repolishing the floor and Boi went about his other duties. It was not until half an hour before lunch-time that Boi realised that the cooker was off and the chicken had not as much as smelt heat. Of course when he was asked, Maina knew nothing about turning off the cooker. What would he want to turn off the cooker for! The big boss was furious about the badly prepared lunch. His wife was even worse.

Meja heard the riot in the house and he questioned the kitchen boy.

'That is nothing,' Maina told him. 'I am a doctor at these little tricks. Just let the big toad keep hopping in my direction.'

36

And the Big Toad did not stop.

A few days later, Boi received a dose of 240 volts electric current from the iron. And of course Maina knew nothing about having damaged it. What did he have to do with the iron? But before the white man came back from his daily tour of the farm, Maina had replaced the live and earth wires in their right places. The wife of the boss was a little more than just mad this time. There was a whole week's washing un-ironed and the iron was in perfect condition. Boi did not know what to make of the incident.

'You could have killed him,' Meja complained to Maina. 'Stop playing tricks on the old man.'

Maina laughed.

'Old man?' he said. 'He should realise he is an old man and stop behaving like a scoundrel. He smashed our door and sat for ages on a coal fire so he can stand anything. Just let him keep crossing my territory.'

Boi did not stop, and incredible as it was he had the boys put on quarter ration. This was a terrible attack as far as Maina was personally concerned and he sat for hours before he could think of the appropriate retaliation. At last he decided. In the kitchen he interchanged the contents of the two containers marked sugar and salt. The bellow that emerged from the farmer at lunch-time that day was heard all over the farm. He threatened Boi with dismissal unless he made use of his numbskull. The old man did not like this at all. He knew he was old and myopic and absent-minded and this might explain the recent accidents in the kitchen. But now his career itself was threatened. And though he could not prove it he knew the boys were somehow involved.

There was a long lull in the battle while Boi thought of the step to take next. During this time life ran on smoothly in the farm and the two young men did their duties in peace and enjoyed full rations.

'This is the way I like it,' Maina said one night as he lay in his bed just after supper.

'What?' Meja asked and blew out the tin lamp.

'Peace of mind, full ration and a friendly atmosphere,' Maina said. 'Don't you like it?'

'I think I do,' Meja said.

'And no more sermons from the wise old man,' Maina added.

A rat moved on the crockery rack.

'Your friends have come,' Meja told him.

'They are your brothers,' Maina told him.

'Brothers indeed,' Meja agreed. 'We share everything including our misery and halved rations. When our rations are slashed they don't have much to collect.'

Maina laughed.

'Have you ever wondered, Meja,' he said, 'what would it be like if we cleaned the utensils after supper one day. What would the rats do?'

'I hate to think of it,' Meja told him. 'Anything could happen. There might be a riot. There might even be a revolution. They might devour us as well as the house. They might even kill each other.'

Maina laughed.

'I am going to clean the plates after supper tomorrow night,' he said. 'Just to see what it will be like, I will clean them.'

'Leave the creatures alone,' Meja told him. 'They don't ask for what we eat. Let them enjoy their meal.'

'Their meal?' Maina laughed. 'They ought to earn it. They ought to work under Boi and then go and beg for their ration from the foreman. I will clean the plates tomorrow night.'

'Don't,' Meja told him.

'I will,' he said.

'Then I won't sleep here,' Meja told him.

'You are free to go,' Maina said. 'Your own hut is still waiting for you out there. I would like to see you sleep there. There are mice too and bed-bugs and fleas and all the miserable little beasts. I will fetch myself a beautiful little baton tomorrow. Then I will clean the plates. If the monsters get into a riot, I will stand back and watch. If the riot gets out of control and they try eating down my hut, I will move in the riot squad, see.'

Meja said nothing. He was sleepy.

'Maybe I will call you to reinforce me if I cannot bash them alone,' Maina told him.

A huge rat scurried across the floor.

'Come prepared for the worst tomorrow,' he said to all. 'I will wash your plates tomorrow. Do you hear me? I will wash the plates tomorrow.'

Meja started snoring softly.

A few weeks later, the storm broke. A number of articles including clothing and a camera had disappeared from the farmhouse. The white man was raving mad. Boi knew nothing about the vanishing clothing and he told him so. Maina and Meja being the closest to the house were summoned and they too knew nothing about the articles. The foreman was called into the case. All he knew about was flour and milk and nothing else, Bwana. The white man was at a loss and was thinking of calling the police when Boi suggested searching the village huts. Quite a bright idea, everybody agreed.

All the village huts were searched by a party organised by the foreman. While the farmer walked around and talked to himself, the soot the bugs and the mice in the huts were turned inside out in the search

38

for the missing property. Eventually the articles were found. They were tied into a nice little bundle and tucked away under a crockery rack, where no one with two eyes myopic or not would have failed to see them. And this hut belonged to the two city youths.

Meja was struck speechless.

Maina swore repeatedly.

'This is a frame up,' he cried. 'We did not steal them. I swear someone placed them there.'

The fat boss watched them, his face flushed with anger.

'Which one of you did it?' he roared.

Meja started to say something then stopped and swallowed loudly. Sweat covered his face.

'Boi did it,' Maina went on to say. 'We did not . . .'

Boi vanished trembling in the direction of the kitchen.

The white man picked up his bundle of possessions.

'Come for your pay when you have packed up,' he said. 'I will take you back to where you were collected.'

He strode back to the farmhouse breathing like a hurt rhino. With hateful glances at the two youths who had angered their master, the rest of the farm hands dispersed.

Maina looked at Meja and shook his head. Meja shrugged. He could hardly speak.

'I told you,' he said hoarsely. 'I told you to stop messing about with the old devil.'

Maina scratched his wavy hair. He too was very shaken by the turn of events.

'Everything has an end,' he said, trying to keep up his carefree mood.

Meja was with him on that one point. Everything has an end. Their guerrilla warfare against Boi was over and their haven of peace lost for ever. They were jobless again and would soon be heading back to the backstreets. No more personal hut, no more home, no more flour and sweet skimmed milk, no more sweet-smelling dust-covered rags for a bed and no more, yes, even Boi. Now that he was leaving, he was sure he would miss Boi as well. And the foreman too. Their bad humour would be forever gone and he was going to miss them.

Maina too stood thinking hard. It never occurred to either of them to plead with the boss to save them the misery of joblessness. They knew he would not listen. If anything, he would beat them up before shoving them back to the city and neither of them wanted to be ill as well as without a job.

'What shall we do now?' Meja asked.

Maina jerked out of his meditations.

'Pack,' he said and walked into the hut.

He stood just inside the door of the hut and looked round. On one side was his bed, rags, nest, he did not know what to think of calling it. On the other side was Meja's collection of the same. And near the door was the rack and its usual load of unwashed tin plates and mugs.

'Pack?' he asked himself and started laughing.

Meja came in and stood next to him. He looked round the hut too and finding nothing unusual turned to his companion.

'What is the matter with you?' he demanded.

'I am just wondering where to start the packing,' the other said.

He walked over to the rack and under it from a small hole, dug out his savings. He counted the money twice before he threw the dirt back into the hole.

'One hundred and fifty-five shillings and eighty-five cents,' he announced. 'How much have you got?'

Meja rolled one of the three rocks at the fireplace aside and from under it extracted a small cocoa tin. Inside the tin were one hundred and seventy-nine shillings and fifteen cents. He did not bother to roll the rock back on to the hole.

'You will not close the world bank?' Maina wanted to know.

'No.'

'Anything else you want to take?'

Meja looked round. He shook his head.

'No.'

'And your favourite tin mug?'

Meja looked at it.

'Give that to Boi. It is a gift from me.'

Maina stopped smiling. He picked the tin mug from the rack where it had sat waiting for the dinner that now would never come. He threw it down to the ground with rage and stamped on it until it was flattened.

The two walked out and left the door wide open for the village mongrels to go in and see for themselves that they had really left. They trooped to the drive of the house where the white man was waiting with the car engine running. Attached to the tail of the car was a trailer waiting to transport their baggage, but when the boss saw that they had no luggage, he did not bother to ask why. He got out of the car and disconnected the trailer.

As the car turned to face down the road, Meja looked out of the window to the lawn. The windmill turned and creaked as always. Meja felt he would miss its creaking too. He knew that he and the windmill shared their burden. They were both driven to the limit of their endurance and all they did was groan and draw water from the stream. The watering bucket too. It now stood in the middle of the lawn where he had left it full of water when the white man had called. It was probably waiting to continue its perpetual journey to the flower beds and its wire handle hung patiently to one side waiting for him. At the sight of the rough wire handle Meja remembered things. He remembered the sound of the music playing on the radio in the white man's home, cool and peaceful, while he toiled in the heat of the day on the lawn. He remembered Boi's call for Maina, sharp and whining and commanding. He remembered the many times he had carried his buckets to the stream. His back and shoulders were hard and solid now, and his legs felt taut as powerful spring traps.

He opened his hands to look at the horny palms. Instead he saw the money which still lay in them, the notes rough and wrinkled and the coins a dull metallic grey.

The car gathered speed and headed for the city.

Meja sat by the ditch and waited, swinging his legs this way and that just above the black dirty water that now flowed there. A few people passed by engrossed in their daily problems and none of them gave the tall lanky youth a thought. But the searching eyes of the young man missed nothing. They scrutinised the ragged beggars who floated ghostly by as closely as they watched the pot-bellied executives wrinkling their noses at the foul stench of the backyards. And between these two types of beings, Meja made comparisons.

But Meja's curiosity was just idle curiosity. He had no pity for the beggars, nor did he envy the executives. He knew too much of what went on among the ragged ones to think of pitying them, and too much of the others to envy their positions. It had taken him two years to learn about human nature. But now he knew: he knew that a beggar given the opportunity could be as mean as a rich man, or even worse.

Since leaving the white man's employment, and exhausting his bank, Meja had gone places and met people. He had talked, eaten, slept and fought with beggars. He had learned all their petty ambitions and all their fears. He had done a lot of things.

He had also tried for the second time to get a job. He went through the same old, old processes he had gone through ages ago when he first left school. He was now more than ever convinced that there was no job anywhere. So he gave up waiting and set about getting used to existing without one. It took a lot of courage and a lot more coaxing from Maina to drive him back to the backstreets.

'See, Meja,' Maina told him. 'There are only two places to go to now; back home or to the backstreets. You cannot live in the air, you know.'

He said nothing.

'Do you want to go home?' Maina asked him.

He shook his head. The thought of going back home did not quite figure out. No. Not before he got that job could it make any sense.

41

'Maybe we shall find another Boi to get us a job,' Maina said, although he knew that that was a bad dream. 'You yourself told me we have got to hang on to what we have got, life. Things will improve. Let us wait and see.'

So they landed back where they had started a little more than two years before. Only this time they were older and wiser. Meja had grown wise in many ways. He had learned that wherever you went even among the beggars, there was always someone to boss you and it did not pay to play about with them. Nor could one afford to annoy the foreman.

As Meja sat by the ditch and watched the world go by, there was no particular thought in his mind. All he wanted was for the days to go swiftly and time to pass, so the day might come when he would either get that job or die. He did not very much care which happened before the other. And right now, it mattered even less. What mattered was that Maina bring the lunch packet soon for he was hungry. And to pass the time while waiting, Meja swung his legs over the mucky water of the ditch this way and that. And he made comparisons among the different species of humanity that flowed by.

He was jerked from his philosophising by a shout from the direction of the back door of the supermarket. Then Maina emerged through the big gates running as though the devil himself was after him. With a heart that threatened to tear its way out of his chest, Meja waited at his station loyally. A tornado of possibilities shot through his mind. He had never seen Maina run so fast in his life and Maina was not one to run for nothing. He came directly at Meja, then swerved to the left. As he passed by, he threw a parcel wrapped in dirty old newspapers and raced on.

'Catch,' he shouted as he went.

Meja's head swam in a confusion of whys and hows as the parcel came sailing through the air, aiming at his chest. He threw out his hands to protect his chest and the parcel landed in them. Then his legs started moving and before he knew it, he was running. He did not know why he was running, only that self-preservation told him to do so and there was nothing else to do now that the object was in his hands.

A man from the supermarket was running after him.

Meja dodged down an alleyway to his right, and the chaser followed screaming at the top of his voice. He turned to the left, keeping in the backstreets. Behind him he saw a large crowd chasing after him headed by a bulky policeman. And now he was frightened and his legs moved faster. His whole body was hot and bathed in sweat. At the top of the street he turned to the left, collided with a beggar and sent him flying into the gutter in a heap of tearing rags. Meja stumbled, nearly fell into a dustbin, dodged it and fled on. He was getting tired now from the exertion and very frightened. He turned to the left a second time.

And he was in the mainstreet.

There were people and cars everywhere and there was no room to run. He stopped petrified by fear. His heart thundered on, his brain clicked into motion but there was no time to decide. His body was numbed and unconsciously he clutched the object to his heaving chest. Salty sweat poured into his mouth and eyes and they ached. Already he could hear his pursuers coming closer. He did not look behind. He knew what was behind him. A mass of charging angry crowd, and a policeman. His cloudy brain said run, and before his reason could respond, his legs were already carrying him up the street as quickly as they could move.

He ran into people and parking meters. He jumped over children on foot and in prams and sent delivery men on to the pavement in a crash of tearing cartons and breaking glass. Somebody made a grab for him and missed. Then everybody was shouting and grabbing at him. His head whirled faster. Panic took hold of him. He snarled and roared defiance as he hit his way through the crowd. Still there was not enough room.

He jumped to cross the street. There was a whoosh of cold air and brakes screamed. A woman screamed and he felt himself flying through the air. Blackness closed over his eyes and there was a frozen thud, thud, thud, in the enveloping darkness. When he reopened his eyes seconds later, he was lying in the middle of the street on a bed of gut-tearing pain. The car was standing a few feet away, a brand new Ford Capri, with a shattered windscreen. Around him people stood and stared. A few women sniffled softly and walked away drying their eyes. The policeman stood inside the encircling crowd and pushed them back.

Meja was still holding the thing Maina had thrown to him in his hands. Now that he was no longer in any hurry he decided to have a look. The parcel was lying in his outstretched hands, and through a wide tear in the wrapping, he looked. He stared at it long and hard. At first he did not believe what he saw. But it was there, as much as the killing pain and everybody was staring at it curiously.

A man dressed in the supermarket attendant's uniform stepped forward and grabbed at the parcel. The wrappings came off and the thing rolled out on to Meja's bloody hands.

Two rotten apples.

The attendant stood transfixed staring at them.

A few flies hovered over them but they seemed more interested in the blood on the hands than the apples.

Everybody watched keenly and not understanding.

Then the attendant moved.

'He had them,' he screamed. 'He had them.'

The crowd held their breath waiting.

The policeman watched the supermarket attendant.

'What?' he asked him.

'The gems, the gems,' the man cried hysterically. 'He stole them from the . . .'

Meja was not interested in what was going on around him. Pain crowded in on him from all sides. The sweet rotten smell of the apples wafted to his dulled senses. It reminded him of something from long days gone by, of the first day he had met his friend in the backstreet. Memories came from the deep, black past and stirred the pain in his body. They increased the pain and it soared to the depth of his soul and he felt weak and spent. Deep in his heart he felt guilty. He had disobeyed and betrayed his companion, Maina. Maina of the backstreets who never complained and never harboured any grudge.

'And whatever you do, keep to the backstreets,' he had told Meja time and again.

Meja felt ashamed and he closed his eyes. The supermarket attendant raved on about gems that never were and down the street an ambulance wailed its way to the scene. But Meja heard none of these. He was very sorry and fast asleep, while pain gnawed at his subconscious mind.

4

MAINA RACED ALONG the backstreets until he came to the main road that skirted the city centre on the western side. He was tired and hot. He stopped running and walked along the main road leading off to the suburbs. He had travelled this same road many times before when going to look for part-time jobs in the suburbs, and now as he walked along he began to relax. He wondered what had prompted the supermarket attendant to run after him. And what had happened to Meja when he raced to the right? Maina decided to let the chase cool off before he went back home. The place would now be full of policemen looking for him, though for what reason he did not understand.

Maina turned up Hill Road. On either side of the road, mansions peeped shyly at him through the hedges and watch dogs stormed up to the gates to snarl at him through the bars. From some houses, beats of cha-cha and soul music floated to the tree-lined road from radios and gramophones. Occasionally whistled tunes also came over the hedges as garden workers busied themselves with the lawns and flower gardens. And where the hedges were low enough, Maina could see the day's washing flaunting proudly white and clean, beating a thudding tune as the wind shook it up and down.

The sun burned hot and the smell of melting tar rose from the surface of the road. Mingled with this was the smell of cooking food as wives prepared lunch for their husbands. This made Maina's stomach turn and complain loudly and he remembered the apples and Meja.

Cars started roaring up along Hill Road as the owners of the houses arrived for lunch. Maina shrank as far away from the road as was possible. Some of the drivers stared at him suspiciously as they turned into their drives and some even got out to close the gates. Maina felt uncomfortable and conspicuous, a moving rag among the trimmed hedges and the big cars. He quickened his pace to get out of the suburbs fast, and his eyes darted here and there, expecting a black uniformed police officer to emerge out of nowhere and take him to the station. The suburbs had been all right when he had come looking for a wood-chopping job. Then he could have lost himself among the fruit vendors. Now with no fruit vendors around, and shaken by his experience in the supermarket, he felt naked and strangely guilty.

He found the man sitting on a corner stone at the junction of Hill

Road and Forest Road. Maina did not give him a thought until the man spoke to him. And he called him by name.

'Maina,' he called.

Maina stopped and stared at the caller. His legs started dancing ready to take off at the slightest hint of danger.

The man was dressed in cheap black jeans, a nylon shirt and a green cotton tie that was almost blue with dirt. His wavy hair was brown with dust and dandruff and it looked as though it had not had any contact with a comb for a long time. His bony cheeks were rough and hard like his black beard, and his eyes were red. When he looked at Maina, Maina felt the eyes go through him and peer into his frightened soul.

'Don't you remember me, Maina?' the man asked.

Maina shook his head. He could not trust his voice not to bring out the fear in him.

'I did not expect you to,' the man went on. 'Are you not Maina?'

Maina nodded.

'It is a long time since we were in school together,' the other told him. 'Do you remember Mang'a and Kimaitho?'

Maina dived into his files of old and new faces but neither the two names nor the face in front of him existed. He shook his head again. All the while he felt uneasiness rise in him.

'But I was learning with you in Standard One,' the other told him.

'Are you Mang'a?' Maina asked hoarsely.

'No,' the other said and laughed.

Maina looked around him suspiciously.

A car came down Forest Road and stopped momentarily as the driver checked Hill Road for oncoming traffic before turning in. He looked at the two men, one sitting the other standing near the corner stone. They were in a very bad position. If a vehicle made the wrong turning those two would be dead.

Maina's companion from the primary school days noticed the driver staring.

'What are you staring at, swine?' he shouted at the driver. 'Keep moving or we will castrate you.'

The driver misunderstood him, waved, smiled and drove on to his lunch.

Maina and the other man watched him go. Then Maina turned round.

'Are you Kimaitho?' he asked.

The other shook his head.

'You called me Kamanda then,' he explained. 'Now they call me the Razor.'

'Who calls you so?' Maina asked.

'My friends,' the Razor answered. 'They are a good lot, those boys. I would like you to meet them. Where are you going now?'

Maina shifted his feet undecidedly. He did not understand how his classmate in Standard One so many years ago could have remembered him. How was he supposed to remember such a classmate? But the man had called him Maina. And he did not look like a policeman. Maina felt he could handle anything but a policeman.

'Nowhere in particular,' he said. 'I was just strolling.'

'In my gang we call it patrolling,' the Razor said and laughed. 'Why did you choose such an awkward name?'

Maina shook his head and his mouth dropped. Suspicion mounted again.

'What are you talking about?' he asked.

'Why, patrolling,' the Razor told him. 'Are you the leader of your gang?'

'Gang?' Maina said.

The Razor stood up.

'Let us talk as we patrol,' he said. 'Who is the leader of your gang?'

'But I don't understand,' Maina said stepping back. 'What gang are you talking about?'

The Razor watched him surprised.

'Don't be afraid,' he said. 'I am not a policeman. I also have a gang and I am not afraid of anything on two legs.'

Maina shook his head.

'I have no gang, and I don't want to have any,' he announced.

The Razor laughed.

'That is the trouble with you people,' he said. 'You haven't yet learned to do things for yourselves. Well, me and my boys, we have. And we are getting on quite well. What are you? Some sort of a labourer?'

Maina shook his head and rubbed the sweat off his face. Then the Razor noticed his plight.

'You mean you don't belong to any gang?' he asked.

Maina nodded. His throat felt dry.

The Razor stopped. He looked him up and down and the corners of his mouth went up.

'You work some place?'

'No.'

'Well, what do you eat? Where do you live? What do you do, man?'

Maina tried to say something then stopped. He opened his mouth again and closed it. He shook his head.

The Razor stared at him, hard.

'You don't work, you don't belong to any gang,' he said. 'What do you do then?'

Maina shrugged.

'Maybe you would like to join the Razors?' the other said.

Maina was even more confused than before.

'That is my gang,' the Razor said. 'Would you like to join us?'

Maina stood undecided. He did not fully understand the gang business but he could already guess. He looked at the Razor again. Slight build, cheap clothes and cheap plastic shoes worn without any socks. Wavy hair and ragged face. He did not look like the type of person to form any good-willed gang. Rather the type for self-help than for public service. Yet, Maina did not know what to do. He was not sure where he was going and the chase from the supermarket was now far behind him. And Meja? Was he still in the back alleys?

'I have a friend,' Maina said.

'He can join us too,' the Razor said. 'Any friend of the Razor's classmate is a friend of the Razor. Where is this friend of yours?'

Maina hesitated. The picture of Meja running away to the right came to his mind. But he would surely be waiting for him behind the supermarket in the evening. It did not occur to him to leave Meja to go and join any sort of organisation alone. They had lived together and he felt lonely when he did not at least know where his friend was. Meja would be waiting for him at their home.

'Where does your friend live?' the Razor asked.

'I left him somewhere,' Maina told him. 'Maybe he is still there.'

The Razor looked at Maina.

'What do you mean maybe?' he asked. 'Is this friend of yours, what do you say, mobile?'

Maina smiled. He was already beginning to relax in the other's company. The free way in which the Razor talked and moved told Maina he could trust him. At the mention of the word 'mobile' Maina visualised Meja flitting from dustbin to dustbin looking for edibles.

'That boy does get to places,' he said. 'Yes, he is very mobile.'

'I like the type,' the Razor said. 'That type of people can get things done when they mean to. Let us go fetch him.'

Maina hesitated.

'What is the matter, man?' the Razor asked. 'Don't you know where he is?'

'No and yes,' Maina said slowly. 'You see, we got into a little trouble this morning and he may be still running.'

'Police?' the Razor asked, apparently uneasy.

'No,' Maina told him.

The Razor relaxed.

'We can't look for him now,' Maina told him. 'Maybe later in the afternoon. He could be anywhere right now.'

The Razor agreed almost too readily, and Maina was glad to note that he was not alone in his police-phobia. They headed for the park to wait for the evening to come. And at the park they lay down under a tree and watched other park-loungers lazily while the Razor told Maina more about his gang workings. In the mid-afternoon when the sun was at its height and the ground all over the park shimmered from the heat, they fell asleep. Maina stretched himself full length and enjoyed a sleep sounder than he had had for a long time. When they woke up in the late afternoon, they were almost all alone in the park.

'It is all right now, I suppose?' the Razor said.

'He should be back now,' Maina told him.

They left the park and entered Forest Road again. They came to the end and turned into Valley Road which eventually led back to the city centre. As they went the Razor talked endlessly about his gang. And as Maina listened, he imagined an enormous gang of underworld crooks holed up in a large hideout, somewhere in the heart of the city. He was a bit eager and nervous. He could not tell what crimes the gang might be involved in. Maybe most of the members were already on the police wanted list. But so long as the gang remained underworld and kept off the mainstreets he would be glad to lose himself in such a crowd. Any gang hide-out was much better than the backstreets. So Maina dreamed of a fairly peaceful future while the Razor poured praise on his gang members. Occasionally he stopped bragging to point out to Maina a strategically placed window or a washline that was close enough to the fence for one to reach over and grab some clothing.

'I could open that window there without trying,' he said. 'Wait.'

They stopped directly opposite the gate as he surveyed the approach to the house and the strategic window. He measured the distance from the gate softly to himself, and the relevant heights and widths.

Maina started feeling uneasy. He knew they were violating some rule though he did not know which.

'Let us go,' he said shakily.

'Yes, I could get in there all right,' the Razor said ignoring him. 'I will ask the boys to have a go at it some time.'

Just then, a giant pug dog came shooting to the gate and stopped just short of it showing its white fangs. It barked and frothed at the mouth but kept its distance. The Razor's face fell.

'That cooks it,' he said starting to move on again. 'Window breaking and frothing brutes do not exactly work out.'

With that remark the Razor ceased talking completely and the two headed away from the suburbs into the city centre. The sun was cooler now and the after-work traffic was just getting to the road-jam point. They walked slowly and carefully among the cars and the homeward bound throng of humanity. It was late when they started into the backstreets. The usual rotting odour hit them and the Razor's nose quivered nervously. Maina noticed this with disappointment. And he quickly led the way to the supermarket. Meja was nowhere near his favourite place by the ditch nor was he to be found anywhere. But Maina, not expecting anything serious to have happened, kept on looking for him among the dustbins.

The Razor watched the desperate search until he could no longer keep his impatience under check.

'What is your friend?' he asked. 'Is he a street sweeper?'

Maina stumbled at the remark and peeped nervously into a dustbin.

'Or is he a reject?' the Razor asked and laughed.

'Uh, what,' Maina stammered, outwitted.

'Where is your friend?' the other asked impatiently. 'Why are you looking into the rubbish bin, he does not live in one of them, does he?'

Maina controlled a mixture of anxiety and fury.

'Let us go,' he said turning round. 'I will look for my friend later.'

The Razor agreed readily and they stepped out of the backstreet into another. How could Maina explain to the knowledgeable Razor that he was not looking for a street sweeper or a reject in a rubbish bin, but for a good friend and at home. He wondered what might have kept his friend away for so long.

They left the city centre again and headed out of town. They walked for a long time and although tired, Maina did not ask where they were going. The Razor seemed to know his way around very well. And he did not mention where they were heading for or where his gang was holed up.

They came to the shanties so abruptly that Maina was stunned by the quick change from the city and its skyscrapers. The shacks were built of paper, tin, mud and anything that could keep out the rain, thrown together in no particular pattern. The shacks were so closely built that from the top of the rise where Maina and the Razor paused to gaze at the view below them, they looked like a rubbish dump full of paper and shining tin. A humming noise floating from the shelters was the only sign that there were people within. Maina held his breath at a sight he would never have thought existed, out of the fiction books he had read at school.

'Welcome to Shanty Land,' the Razor said with a new confident voice.

Maina nodded absent-mindedly.

'Everybody here knows the Razor and any classmate of the Razor is a friend of theirs.'

Maina nodded again.

They descended the slope into the valley of the shanties. The air was heavy with the smell of smoke, urine and countless other odours. There was one very familiar smell that now met Maina: the smell of human beings, as he remembered it from the farm, warm and very relaxing. Maina felt the backstreet tension wear off and it was replaced by a feeling of discovery as he squeezed his way through the narrow streets, following his guide. Every now and then the Razor called into one of the hen-houses and a voice answered from the depths of paper and smoke. The few people who saw them stared at Maina like a new strange animal, only to look away when the Razor glared at them. Some distance into the heart of the shanties, the Razor entered one of the paper-walled huts and left Maina waiting outside. There were some murmurings from within and someone, a woman, laughed loudly.

'Come in, Maina,' the Razor called out.

Maina paused, then bent almost double, crawled into the hut. It was dark inside and he could hardly see. He rubbed his eyes and dimly saw figures which he took to be people. Some of them were smoking and the whole place was filled with smoke as of burning grass. Among the dimly visible smoking people, Maina could not recognise even the Razor. He stood by the door peering into the gloom waiting for someone to tell him what to do or where to go next.

'You will see better if you move away from the door,' a rough voice said.

Maina assumed the address was meant for him and stepping to one side stepped on someone's bare foot.

'Hey, are you blind or deaf or something?' the hurt party complained.

Maina murmured an apology and looked round again. This time, from the light that managed to dodge its way through the mud and paper streets, he saw the occupants of the hut more clearly. There were eight of them sitting on crates all round the room, while the Razor sat on the only bed. There was a woman lying on the bed, staring at Maina with open curiosity. The Razor sat with one arm round her shoulders. All the others watched Maina quietly.

'Who is he, Razor?' the girl asked.

'A friend of mine,' the Razor said to her. 'His name is Maina.'

The others in the room kept quite quiet.

'Maina,' the Razor went on. 'Meet the gang. Sitting on the right there, the mono-eyed one, is the Crasher. On his left is Professor. Next to him is the Sweeper and the other is . . .'

Maina followed the introductions round the hut. As names were matched to faces his interest in the gang members rose. The one-eyed Crasher was thin and frail and did not look like he could crash an egg with a ten pound mallet. He was dressed in a faded red or brown sports-shirt and old jeans much like the Razor's. His chin was clean-shaven, his hair dirty and wavy, and his claw-like fingers clutched at a thick cigar which produced a foul, dark cloud of smoke. His one good eye watered from the smoke and he kept rubbing away the tears with the back of a bony hand. Between the drying and the watering again, the one eye watched Maina as meanly as a snake's.

The Professor was also smoking a cigar like the others. His head was almost bald, although from the look of what remained of him, he was a young man. His chin sported a sharp pointed beard which had probably earned him his name. He was also roughly dressed and his ears stuck out of his head like a scarecrow's. His head reminded Maina of the turnips grown in Boi's farm, with the ears standing for the leaves.

The Sweeper was a thick-set middle-aged man, the oldest in the gang. His cheeks were fat and he had a gap between his front teeth. His bomb-shaped head and huge shoulders gave him the appearance of a charging bull. His gapped brown teeth, scanty moustache and massive bulk reminded Maina of the gigantic rats at the farm which invaded their hut nightly.

'And right here next to me is the Razor's own heart,' the Razor finished the introductions and hugged the girl with one arm. 'Her name is Sara.' He kissed her forehead.

Maina glanced around again and gave the gang another look over. His picture of a well-organised gang and a peaceful hideout went right out of focus. All he could see was a lot of desperately poor people trying their best to hold on to the only thing they had in the world, Life. A very pitiable lot indeed, but they did not seem to be suffering from self pity. They seemed to be getting along with their dark little hole and their fat cigars very well.

'How do you like the gang?' the Razor asked Maina. 'I must agree they don't look intelligent, but that is only because they are not trying to. They are a very jolly crowd.'

Maina fought to extract himself from his reflections.

'I am glad to have met them,' he said.

'But we don't even want to know you,' the Sweeper said standing.

'What?' the Razor shot from the bed.

The Sweeper looked the Razor up and down, a puny little creature in comparison to his own bulk. Then he threw his fat cigar to the ground and ground his hoof on it.

'What did you say?' the Razor asked again, his hands hanging menacingly by his sides.

'You brought us an old friend of yours a year back,' the Sweeper said. 'We all ended up in jail and two of us were hanged. How do we know this friend of yours is not a spy like the other?'

'I am the Razor,' the other said. 'I decide who joins the gang and who does not. Right? If you feel you want to have a say in what I do, you form your own gang and lead them to hell. And this applies to anyone else in the room who too might be getting big headed.'

He looked round the hut challengingly. Most of the gang looked

away when they met his gaze. It was open though, that they did not
agree with him.

'But Razor,' Sara spoke up unexpectedly. 'We must be reasonable.
The security of the gang counts before all else.'

The Razor spun round.

'You too in this? Take my advice,' he told her. 'You speak when I
ask you to or get out.'

Sara put on her most innocent look.

'I did not mean to annoy you,' she said, rising from the bed.

She was wearing an extremely short skirt and her thick thighs
showed more than could be called decently. Her huge breasts pushed
her blouse out in front of her so hard it looked like it would rip and
spill them on to the floor. Studying her carefully, Maina decided that
though she could not be called beautiful, she was as much a woman
as any. She walked up to the Razor and slipped her hand in his. She
was shorter than he was but made up with breadth.

'We like your friends, Razor,' she said as sweetly as she could make
it. 'What we don't want is another disaster. We have been together for
over four years now. It would be sad if a good friend of yours wrecked
us. Don't you think so?'

The Razor glanced at Maina.

The Professor wriggled uncomfortably.

'We had a meeting while you were away,' he said hesitantly, looking
around for support from the others.

The Razor jerked and pushed Sara away.

'A what?' he screamed. 'Who said you could hold meetings in my
gang when I was not in? Tell me that. Whose idea was it?'

Nobody spoke. Tension hung in the atmosphere and some of the
gang members started trembling. The Sweeper sat down, glad that
someone had diverted the Razor's storm from himself. Professor
fingered his beard nervously.

'Who was it?' the Razor asked trying to control his anger.

Again nobody spoke.

'Was it you, Crasher?' he turned to face the praying-mantis that was
Crasher.

Crasher shook his head without looking up.

'Sweeper?'

'Not me, Razor.'

'Professor?'

'We were . . .' Professor started to say.

'Professor?' Razor cut him short.

'No, sir.'

Everybody shook their heads or grunted a negative until only Sara
remained unquestioned.

The Razor eyed her questioningly.

'It wasn't quite a meeting,' she explained. 'We were just talking and it came to the memories of Chief. You remember he was killed when your good friend talked on us. So . . .'

The Razor reached into his pocket and pulled out a dangerous looking flick knife. Its razor shone dimly, long and sharp like the tongue of a venomous snake. Everybody in the hut except Maina froze in their places. Sara's word froze in her mouth and her face looked pale and scared. The Crasher choked on his cigar's smoke and nearly fainted trying to stop from coughing and attracting the Razor's attention. Even the big Sweeper it seemed was afraid of the smallish knife.

The Razor looked round at the frightened people with satisfaction.

'I am reminding you,' he said slowly and with authority. 'I am the leader in this gang. I will be present in any get-together of any size in future.'

Nobody moved.

'If I say anybody is a friend, he is a friend,' he went on. 'And that is enough.'

Again he paused and waited for any complaint and of course there was none.

'Maina here is a classmate of mine and he is to join the gang,' he concluded.

Sara broke the spell.

'You mean you went to school?' she asked, excitedly.

'I wouldn't lie to you, now would I?' the Razor said, relaxing too. 'Ask Maina if you don't believe me, I was a good scholar too.'

Everybody looked up at Maina and tension decreased. The events of the past ten seconds or so had Maina confused. Now he felt uncomfortable as well.

'Tell them, Maina,' the Razor ordered.

Maina hesitated. He did not feel it right to admit right there and then that he had never met the so-called Razor until today. After what everybody had just gone through it would be a very serious letdown for the Razor. And the thought of the little dangerous knife reappearing, this time for him, was very unpleasant. Everybody was waiting eagerly.

'Yes,' Maina said desperately.

'You see,' the Razor said, relieved. 'He was my classmate. Give him a smoke, Sweeper,' he ordered.

The Sweeper started searching in his pockets. The Razor's knife disappeared back into his pocket and conversation started flowing again. The Razor swept Sara off her feet and carried her back to the bed. There they lay necking as though nothing had happened. The other gang members set about minding their own business and let the Razor mind his, Sara.

The Sweeper found a thick cigar and offered it to Maina. He also invited him to sit on the floor by him as all the crates were occupied. At the first pull on his cigar, Maina choked and coughed until his chest ached. But as all the others were smoking the same brand of thick fat cigars and seemed to enjoy it, he chose to pretend that he liked it all the same. Anyway, anything the Crasher or the Professor could stand, Maina could stand three times over, he told himself. He smiled at the Sweeper and nodded. The Sweeper did not smile back. After a few more drags, Maina felt more relaxed and comfortable. The smoke no longer felt sharp and suffocating. It was warm and flat and pleasant. Its smell was now sweet and through the smoke he was able to converse with even the Sweeper more easily.

Maina finished the first one and the Sweeper offered him another. The two talked a lot and the fact that he did not know what they were talking about did not seem to matter. What mattered was that he was among friends. He felt that he had known the Razor and the Sweeper and everybody else for a long time and he liked and smiled at everyone, even the mean one-eyed Crasher. The dim light of the hut was comforting, making the rough unswept floor look smooth and feel smooth to his bottom. The walls looked clean and beautiful and he had never been happier in his life.

On the bed, the Razor started undressing first Sara and then himself. Maina watched and smiled in an amused way as the two dived under the only blanket, among the beautiful-looking sacks on the bed. Then the Razor's head emerged again.

'By the way, Maina,' he said smiling, 'feel at home among friends.'

'Sure, Razor, sure,' Maina said in a drugged voice.

And nobody seemed bothered by what went on around them. They all sat and smoked bhang, warm, free and contented. They were one neatly bound gang, bound with love, rough living and lawlessness. Nothing mattered outside the circle. The fact that poverty and ignorance dwelt among them was insignificant. Nobody noticed the overcrowdedness in the little hut nor the near-nakedness of his companions, nor even the fact that they had no personal possessions nor even a fireplace. Nobody wondered what they were going to eat for supper or where they were going to sleep on the dusty floor. What they had, they shared equally and unselfishly: conversation, bhang, human togetherness and, yes, a little poverty too. Between the paper walls that was all.

Outside the hut, dust stirred by the evening winds swept down the shanty lanes carrying with it the smell of urine and dirty bodies. The crackling of a hungry hen, the cry of a hungry baby and the hum of subdued voices were wafted away, leaving the rubbish dump that was Shanty Land calm and peaceful.

Life in the gang was an uphill job for Maina for at least the first few weeks. He had to learn from scratch what it took to keep alive and out of prison and still eat and drink. He had to learn the tricks one by one: all the tricks he had feared to try before he lost himself among the backstreets and the dustbins. He was taught how to pick pockets, pick wrist watches and snatch bags without causing a stampede in the crowded mainstreets. He learned how to open closed windows and doors with his eyes closed and also how to carry off a whole wash-line plus the washing while the owner was whistling in the kitchen only a few yards away. Most of his theory was taught by the experienced Razor himself, assisted by the Crasher who seemed very well informed about the petty little tricks that kept the light in the little hut burning. Maina taught himself to like the Crasher and benefited a great deal from the friendship. The only person he could never exactly come to like was the Sweeper. The Sweeper did not even try to like Maina and this did not help the others' efforts.

When it came to the real thing, Maina was scared. The idea of having to snatch a bag and run for it was very terrifying. Maina even had the mind to resign from the gang forthwith. But going back to the backstreets after being away for so long did not sound very sensible. He could not tell where Meja had got to, for he had looked for him without success behind the supermarket on a few occasions. He wondered whether Meja had at last decided to go back home and explain his failure to his people. At times when the life in the gang seemed very bleak, Maina wondered whether he too should not have gone home and tried to explain to his family. But deep inside he knew it would take a lot of telling to make his illiterate family understand how he, a man who had squandered all his ageing father's treasury in going to school, had failed to scratch himself a living. Was it not true that people went to school to read and write and become wise? And was it not also true that well-read people got jobs after school and earned a lot of money? How could he dare then to go and preach that he had failed to get even a badly paid job? How could he? How?

So the best he could do was stick around a gang of crooks and hope that some day he would end up in a better life.

Meanwhile, life whirled on around him, in Shanty Land and the whole city and the world, indifferent to his education and his hopes. All round him people were being born, others going to school, others getting sacked from their jobs, and yes, some were being employed too.

Life in the little shelter in the heart of Shanty Land did not change much. The place was dark and dank and badly aired. The Razor lay on the kingly bed with his queen, Sara. The rest of the gang lay about on crates, and on the dusty floor, that had never been swept since the creation. And as usual, everybody was minding his own business, be it a short stab of bhang, beard-stroking or, for the few who had advanced that far, looking for lice on their clothes.

'Maina,' the Razor called suddenly.

'Yes,' Maina answered looking up from mending his shirt with a stolen bit of thread and a microscopic needle.

'Are you hungry, Maina?' the other asked.

'Yes, very hungry,' Maina said unsuspectingly.

'So am I,' the Razor told him.

Maina puzzled over that one. But then thinking it was the usual drugged talk, he bent back to his work.

'Would you like to eat, Maina?' the other went on.

'Sure,' Maina said and smiled.

'So would I,' the Razor told him. 'So would everybody.'

Then he sighed.

'How would you like to get us something to eat, Maina?' he asked.

Maina jerked his head up. At last, he told himself, this was the moment he had dreaded most ever since his training started. The examination had at last come, and now he had to prove his worth. He scratched his head in confusion.

'But I don't understand,' he said innocently as he could make it without uncovering his fright.

'I will tell you in Italian,' the Razor told him. 'Everybody has had a go at getting us food at one time or the other. You have only eaten and learned. Now you know. We all would like to eat. It is your turn.'

Maina looked round the dark hut. The Professor was crooning over his dirty nails, uninterested. He ate when he saw others eat and you could never catch him thinking about food. You were lucky if you caught him thinking at all. He did what the Razor ordered, did it well, and went back into oblivion. The Crasher was dozing although he had not done much else for over a week. He loved dozing, and the most sensible explanation he could give to anyone who might have been interested was that he was in love with sleep. One does not stay away from his lover. One of the gang members was playing hide and seek with lice on his tattered clothes. Most of the others were smoking their endless stock of bhang. Only the Sweeper was interested and he sat watching Maina with an amused smile on his lips.

'I understand that,' Maina said turning to the Razor, 'but I don't know what to do. Where shall I get the food?'

'That is your nightmare,' the Razor said and rolled on his side on the bed to pet Sara's breasts. 'What we want is food. Whether you dig it up some place or vomit it we are not interested. Are we, Pet?'

'No,' Sara said as expected.

Maina stood up helpless. He put on his shirt, the mending forgotten. The Sweeper watched and the amused smile enlarged into a big-faced grin.

'You want some sound advice, friend?' he asked.

Maina turned round eagerly.

'Why don't you try raiding the kitchen department of the Oriental Hotel?' the Sweeper advised.

Maina's scanty biceps contracted and his face felt hot. He looked the Sweeper up and down and wished he had been smaller. Just a bit smaller than he was. Most of the gang laughed at the Sweeper's advice. The Professor laughed loud too, then turned to his partner.

'What did he say?' he asked.

'I was not listening,' his neighbour told him.

The Razor looked over his head at the laughing crowd. Then he pushed the girl away and got out of bed. He stood surveying the members of the gang from one to the other, his hands perched on his slim hips.

'I do not think that was funny at all,' he told them. 'You fools think it is funny because you have never given it a thought before. None of you had the guts. And then you laugh.'

Everybody got busy minding his own business. No one spoke. Even the Sweeper looked down at the unswept floor, and his horny nails. The Razor turned to Maina.

'What you mean is that you don't know where to get the food?' he asked.

Maina nodded.

'And if you are told what to do, you will do it?'

He nodded again.

The Razor looked round the hideout again weighing up his followers to find out which of them was most suitable for the job. They kept their eyes down and tried their best to look incapable. Some did not even have to try.

'Sweeper,' the Razor called. 'Go with him.'

The other flew to his feet, the grin disappearing.

'What?' he bellowed.

'You heard me,' the leader told him.

The Sweeper was nearly exploding with fury and hate. He seemed to have suddenly grown very tall and very gigantic.

'But . . . but this is against the rules,' he raved. 'A new member has to prove his worth even before he is trained. That was how I joined.'

'And what were you then,' the Razor asked. 'What were you before you joined?'

The Sweeper twitched and his face became uglier with bitterness.

'Hungry, ill and wanted by police,' the Razor told him. 'That is what you were before I allowed you to join the gang, Sweeper. Now you have grown into a bull and you want to . . .'

'But you made the rules,' the Sweeper complained. 'I did not.'

'That is right, Sweeper,' the Razor told him. 'I made the rules and I still do. Maina here is a classmate of mine and he is not wanted by police. I wonder whether they are still looking for you for that rape.'

The Sweeper jumped up and stamped his foot. The whole hut was now awake and trembling. With closed fists, the Sweeper approached the Razor.

It happened like by magic. One minute it was not there, the next minute the dangerous little knife materialised in the Razor's bony hand. That checked the Sweeper's movement. He stopped and stared at the little thing, his mouth producing a trickle of saliva that ran down his chin on to his bare hairy chest.

'Go on, try it,' the Razor said, smiling with savage pleasure. 'Come. I will cut your face into beautiful ribbons for you.'

The Sweeper looked helpless. His muscles were still tense and his fury shook him in spasms. He turned round and smashed his fist into the Crasher who fell down moaning. His fury was still not expended. He turned and looked at the sharp razor again. It still looked shiny and dangerous. His whole body trembled.

'Get out,' the Razor said and stepped forward, his knife held expertly in front of him.

The Sweeper stepped back, his hands held in the defensive position.

'Out,' the Razor said again.

'I . . . am sorry,' the Sweeper said trembling, and it was clear to all now that the great Sweeper was licked.

The Razor stepped closer and stabbed the air in front of the big man's stomach. Had it been his intention to do it, he could have gutted him with that one sweep.

'I did not mean it,' the other said moving backwards. 'I am sorry, Razor . . . I am sorry . . . I am sorry.'

The Razor had never looked more dangerous.

'I said get out of here,' he snarled. 'You have caused a lot of trouble in my gang. Get out and stay out. Anybody who does not like a friend of the Razor does not enter this place.'

The Sweeper trembled helplessly and sweat flowed over his fat face. He could not go. Without the leader he would be helpless. They all knew it. The Razor to them meant a person who could think out things. A person who could keep them in one gang, a gang that still functioned while the others were cooling off in prison. Few had thought it wise to desert the Razor. The Sweeper could not leave the band and hope to live long on his own. He wagged his head, wrung his hands and pleaded.

But the Razor was not listening.

'Go out, one,' he counted. 'Go out, two. Go out, three . . .'

The Sweeper remembered the countless other gangsters he had seen walk out of this same hut with their faces bleeding and in tatters. He grunted defeatedly and headed for the door.

'Wait,' the Razor ordered.

He stopped and stood without turning back. Waiting.

'Maina,' the Razor called. 'Go with him.'

Maina stirred and came back to reality. On frozen legs he started for the door. The Razor addressed the Sweeper.

'If you don't show him what to do, don't bother to come back.'

The two walked from the hut into the dusty shanty afternoon. Hens scratched lazily in the dust for food and the mongrels lay on the dust and watched the two men pass by. The sun was hot and there were few people moving. Only the ragged tots raced around in their usual pastime of racing one another. Once an army of children was seen crowded along a lane chasing after an old ragged, tennis ball, probably the only tennis ball in the whole of Shanty Land.

As he led the way around huts, hens and groups of children, the Sweeper complained incessantly about having to look after every other bastard that joined the gang, while no one had taken care of him when he first arrived.

'I am very sorry,' Maina said.

The Sweeper stopped in mid-step. He turned on him.

'You know I did not even want to know you,' he said sourly.

'You heard what the Razor said,' Maina reminded him.

The Sweeper stared at him and hated him. He spoke through clenched brown teeth that had a gap in the middle. His thick tongue spat poison.

'For heaven's sake don't you ever threaten me,' he drawled.

Just then the Professor caught up with them, breathless and sweaty. He was still dressed in the tight old jeans and his toes peeped through his shoes.

'The Razor said I go with you,' he explained to the uninterested men.

The Sweeper glanced at him and snarled, and the gap between his dirty brown teeth made him look even more like the charging rats at the farm. He led the way towards the city centre.

Fear of policemen and shouting crowds hung over his head as Maina followed the two veteran crooks into the city mainstreets. Right among the crowds he feared, Maina moved with the others while they patrolled.

But he was so busy controlling his terror that he did not utilise the tactics he had been taught only theoretically. He felt that the eye of every citizen, every passing policeman and the whole city was watching his every move. Dodging his way around people became a nerve-tearing task. But he managed to keep with the other two as they hunted for the right prey.

When the victim was spied and marked they followed him here and there as he did his shopping, praying that he did not exhaust his purse before they had a go at relieving him of its contents. He was a male of a medium build, dressed in a blue suit and brown shoes. In fact it was while he was paying a shoeshine boy that this thick bundle of notes was discovered. Immediately, he was pointed out to Maina.

'There is your bird,' the Sweeper murmured. 'Don't lose him; he is really loaded.'

Maina was now really terrified.

'What am I to do?' he asked.

The Sweeper nearly fainted at the question. Then he recovered quickly and smiled slyly.

'Why,' he said sarcastically, 'walk right up to him, shake his hand and say, "Please, sir, dear sir I want to pick your pocket!"' Then he became serious and deformed his face in contempt. 'Don't be foolish,' he said. 'My orders were to show the Razor's, uh, classmate what to do.'

The Professor bumped in.

'Really it is easy,' he encouraged. 'Just brush past him and flick in your hand thus.' His hand shot in and out of Maina's pocket in a flash and pulled out the dirty rag that passed for a handkerchief.

But the man's money was in his inside coat pocket and not as easily accessible. They followed him for some time looking for an opportunity, and meanwhile Maina prayed that the man might go into a shop and never come out again, or even be inexplicably picked up by a police patrol car or a helicopter or anything to put him out of reach. This would save Maina the torment of knowing that sooner or later, he would have to reach right next to the bulky man's huge heart and extract the wad of notes. The idea of getting caught at it was so terrifying that Maina fell back for a brief moment and the others caught up with him.

'What is the matter with you, man?' the Sweeper asked.

'I can't,' he answered mournfully. 'He is moving too fast.'

The Sweeper looked him up and down, from his trembling legs to his sweaty brow.

'What then, coward,' he enquired. 'Shall I report to the Razor that his classmate funked?'

Maina nodded and his throat felt dry. He wished that the ground would open and swallow him right there and then.

'It is hopeless,' he moaned. 'He is moving too fast.'

'It is not wise to let him go,' the Professor ventured. 'Try to keep up with him. You must get that money.'

'Run after him if you must,' the Sweeper suggested. 'You are even allowed to hit him. This is your show.'

Maina quickened his pace and almost stumbled after the blue-suited man. In his heart fear of policemen and prisons and the gang and the Razor gnawed at him. He thought of running all the way back to the backstreets and diving into the safety of the first dustbin he came to, but he did not know which part of the city he was in and he dreaded the thought of getting lost among so many people. The crowds might get excited. He might run into a policeman. Anything could happen in the mainstreets.

Desperately he staggered after their prey, fear crawling on his skin. He was so confused that he made directly for the white man. They came to a bus stop and just then, a bus stopped. The blue suit headed for the door of the bus, and for a fleeting second, Maina nearly screamed with rage and nervousness. Before he could help himself his hands made a grab for the man's coat tails. He missed and the man vanished into the interior of the protective bus. People jostled around him and Maina was really scared. They shoved him towards the door of the bus and it was all he could do to stop from crying out in hurt rage and desperation. Just as the bus was starting to move off, the Sweeper and the Professor who had stopped and watched the whole episode ran up. The three of them bustled into the bus and headed for the suburbs. The bus conductor came round and Maina's head went into a complete black-out. The Sweeper dug into his rags and miraculously produced a few weathered coins. He paid for the three of them, then opened the window of the bus for Maina to get some air. He would need all his senses around him now that he was going to work out of the protective cover of the mainstreet crowds. He was sure going to need them.

The blue suit alighted a few miles on. The three shadows also got off. There were a few people round the bus stop and this was a bad omen just in case there was going to be a struggle. Then the last stroke fell. Their victim headed straight for a mansion directly opposite the bus stop. And the three Razors stood paralysed. Maina glanced at his two helpless companions as their prey walked into the drive of his house, carrying his purchases as well as their money, their food and their life. And he was whistling happily to himself.

'Get him,' the Sweeper growled, shoving Maina after the man. 'If he gets lost, you are done for.'

Maina stumbled a few steps after the blue suit and the gravel under his feet complained. He hesitated for a moment and looked back. His two companions were standing facing the opposite direction as though they had nothing to do with him at all. And hanging in the atmosphere around them, Maina saw the Razor's sparkling blade.

He started after the blue-suited man as though in a dream. He did not know what to do or where to go next. Only to walk away from the crooks and away from the blade that hung over their heads.

He came to the front door of the house through which the man had just disappeared. The man was still whistling and without caring to look back or to close the door behind him, he threw his packages on a sofa and took off his coat. Then he hung it on a chair, and picking up the packages again, walked through another door calling for someone. Maina's heart thundered into life and his head ached from concentration. Right there on a chair hung the coat inside whose pocket lay the wallet he had followed so far and for so long. For a moment, he was immobile and undecided. Then he heard the owner of the house coming back along the corridor and he exploded into life. He charged into the room. He upset a chair that went crashing to the floor. He grabbed the coat eagerly and headed back for the door.

Just then the owner of the coat reappeared. In a flash he took in what was happening and gave a cry. He grabbed the upset chair and sent it flying after the thief. A second too late. The chair smashed into the glass door and broke itself into pieces on the frame.

Out at the bus stop, the waiting passengers looked round at the noise and saw the thief come flying down the drive. Quickly they fanned across the entrance to the drive cutting off escape that way. Maina saw this and altered course. He headed for the back of the house, dodging round flower bushes and washing lines. At the back was a five-foot high thorn hedge and beyond it thick bush and freedom. The hedge had been recently pruned and the sharp stabs stood menacingly facing inwards at Maina. He had never done any sports anywhere but he was going to get away at any cost. Without any hesitation, he took three long steps and jumped. He hit the hedge full force, a force that landed him on the other side much bruised and torn. He was still clinging to the coat and picking himself up he headed deeper into the bush. The Sweeper and Professor were already waiting for him there. He practically collapsed into their arms and they dragged him deeper under cover. Through gasping for breath and trying to focus his mind on what he had just accomplished, Maina felt his friends patting him on the back and congratulating him enthusiastically. But his mind was still spinning. Spinning in fear, fear of policemen, running crowds and, – and the Razor's cold, heart-chilling blade.

5

FOR THE FIRST TIME in a long time, there was merriment and feasting in the little drab hut in the middle of Shanty Land. The floor was free of dust and life ran much faster than usual. Food littered the floor and talk flowed as freely as the Nubian Gin in the little white bottles. The gang devoured the food efficiently and savagely and talked in grunts, their cheeks filled to bursting point. Every now and then, one of the gang paused between mouthfuls and drunkenly expressed his heartfelt congratulations to Maina the hero of the century. They had never owned so much money, nor so much food and drink in their lives, and they said so.

Maina was happy about the whole thing although the bruises hurt him a great deal. He was happy that he had made even those of the gang members who had not shown the insides of their mouths for a long time smile with satisfaction. Rather they did not exactly smile, but as they opened their mouths to shovel in more edibles, in that split second when their jaws were not busy destroying the texture of the food, they nodded to Maina. The point was that they were happy, though they had never learned to say thank you in their lives. Even the Sweeper was happy and thankful. And Maina thought he saw Sara darting little admiring glances in his direction. Most of all Maina was happy that he had come through the mission more or less in one piece – but for the little bits of flesh left hanging like tiny flags on the sharp thorn hedge.

The merriment reached its climax when someone suggested a speech from someone to thank Maina for his beautiful bit of life-saving work. The Professor rose and tried his hand at delivering one. He failed because he was too drunk to keep on his feet long enough to reach the main point. He first went on a detour and told a tale about Maina struggling with the whole family, and how he had come in to rescue his gallant friend single handed. The Sweeper accused him of lying and they nearly came to blows. Then the Crasher tried his oratorical powers. He did not get very far either. He was so full of love and admiration for Maina that he could not help crying drunkenly and his one eye rained so many tears he could not continue. He did not get around to thanking Maina either.

While speech-making was going on, the Razor invited Maina to take a sip from the Nubian Gin bottles. Up to now Maina had not come to be a fan of such strong stuff, and bhang he smoked only when he had to and there was nothing else to do. Now in a burst of bravado he accepted the Razor's offer and took a sip from the bottle. It was bitter and burned his throat so that he refused any more.

'Come on, try some more,' the Razor encouraged. 'It is good for health.'

Everybody in the hut agreed that it was a good idea for everybody to drink and toast everybody else. But Maina shook his head, holding at his throat.

'Look, do it this way,' the Razor said and threw most of the contents of the bottle down his own throat.

He handed the bottle to Maina. Maina looked at the vicious liquid, holding it up to the little evening light that came shyly through the door. He shook his head.

Sara solved the problem. She produced a few coins and sent the Sweeper off on a secret errand. He brought back a bottle of Fanta and everybody gave a cheer. Sara tenderly mixed a drink for Maina, one that was a little more agreeable. Maina looked at the encouraging eager faces all round him then swallowed the drink quickly. It was by now dark outside and for the first time the gloom became intolerable. Not that there ever was more light before, but then there never was so much food and drink to get rid of either. And everybody wanted to see everybody else's smiling face and be happy. The Professor then performed the miracle of the day. He produced a dirty little stab of a candle and lit it. The door was thrown screeching back, and in the candle light, love blossomed among the Razors.

Soon, very soon, Sara's purchases of food were annihilated and the leftovers, which were few, were thrown into a corner to rot. Everybody's attention was now turned to the little gin bottle and a contented song or two were hummed in the background. Even Maina now drank freely straight from the bottle. His senses were numbed like those of the rest and when somebody produced a thick stub of bhang he applauded with the others. The hallucinating cigar was passed from one set of wet lips to the other. Sara too took part in the ritual just as she had done with the spirit. Talk rose higher and Maina's drunken senses were aroused in warning.

'Sh . . . sh . . . sh,' he said and hiccuped. 'That . . . that talk is too . . . too loud. Someone might hear.'

The truth was that just at that minute, their voices could have been received by the earth's satellites without any antennae and no need of a transmitter. Most of the Shanty Land citizens heard it but none dared go anywhere near the Razor's hut unasked. The gang was unperturbed.

'You are still afraid?' the Razor laughed. 'Relax, my friend. This place is the heavenly Shanty Land. I am the king, no soldiers, no police, no nothing. Nothing at all to fear. Drink and speak as loud as you like. I am boss Razor here, isn't that so, boys?'

They screamed applause. At last somebody had made a speech that made sense.

Maina smiled uneasily. The fat cigar was passed round for the hundredth time and a song sprang up from nowhere: the filthiest song Maina had ever heard sung. It was conducted by the Crasher, his one eye dancing with excitement, supported by the Sweeper, and the rest of the gang joined in the chorus, except Maina, the Razor and his heart, Sara, and the stupidly drunk Professor. The song rose to a crescendo of hard broken voices then fell to stillness. They had another go at making it a success then gave up altogether. Quarrels broke out among the most friendly of the gang members, but none were sober enough to stage a real fight. After a few vain attempts at throwing blows and tossing bottles around, the tired warriors gave up and leaned lazily back on the wall of the hut. The spirit-soaked cigar was passed round for the millionth time and its intoxicating smoke filled the room. The only sober thing in the room was the small candle that burned solemnly at the neck of an empty gin bottle, throwing drunken shadows everywhere.

The Razor staggered to his feet and followed by Sara went out of the hut to urinate on its wall next to the door. He had had enough of the celebrations and now, still followed by Sara, he came back and the two got on to the noble bed to flirt drunkenly. Most of the gang sat back and dreamed of a satisfied future, a future full of food and beer and cigarettes and happiness. Few of them indeed had ever seen the inside of a real bar in their lives.

The merry-making went on late into the night. The gin was exhausted and some people went back to tilting the already empty ones in an attempt to get at least a few drops. Someone accidentally swallowed the diminishing cigar stub and there was not much else left for the gang to do but to sit back and live.

Then suddenly someone was holding a bottle full of gin. At the announcement of the discovery everybody jolted to full wakefulness again.

'Who has been hiding drink like that?' the Crasher said, trying to focus his eye on the bottle. 'Here, let me have a swig.'

He grabbed the bottle from the discoverer and a struggle ensued. The noise increased and this excited the Sweeper. He erupted into action so fast it took the other two by surprise. He pulled the trouble makers apart and tossed them into a corner to continue their argument there, minus the bottle. Then he held the bottle to the light of the candle and saw that it was almost full. Before he could taste it the two fighters counter-attacked in a combined force and sent him to the ground sprawling. The Crasher then grabbed the bottle and poured most of its contents down his own throat. Then suddenly he pulled the bottle from his mouth and spat furiously. This checked the others attack and they watched curiously in mid step. He smelt at the neck of the bottle and twisted his face disgustedly.

'What sort of spirit is this?' he asked looking very worried.

The Sweeper extended his hand.

'Let me see,' he said.

He held the bottle to the candle light again and this time noticed that the remaining liquid was a little yellow in colour. He shook his head and smelt the contents. He screwed his head to one side, thought for a second and then had another little sniff. He handed the bottle back to the frightened Crasher and collapsed on the floor twisting and roaring with laughter.

His room-mates watched him curiously, and the Crasher took another sniff. The Razor bounded from the bed, grabbed the bottle and smelled at its contents. He also gave it back to the owner and fell back on the bed laughing. Then one by one the gang sniffed at the liquid and everybody screamed with laughter. Only Crasher stood in the middle of the hut holding his hard earned bottle, and grinning drunkenly.

'Go on,' the Sweeper said to him through fresh outbursts of mirth. 'Drink, Crasher. Drink to your health and satisfaction. Fill your tummy with stinking yellow urine. Go on, drink.'

The Crasher's face went through an amazing change. Horror, shame and drunkenness turned the idea on his face into an unknown coded expression. He was angry, ashamed and drunk all in one well-stirred mess. He whirled the bottle over his head with rage and sent it flying through the paper wall to break in hundreds of pieces on the hard ground outside. During this frenzied whirling he accidentally emptied the remaining urine over his head and body. Then he fell to the floor moaning and retching and drunkenly beating the floor with his closed fists.

Maina had up to now been laughing half-heartedly. Now he doubled up, loosened his vocal chords and showed the boys that he could laugh. He too had a voice. He then changed into high frequency and let out a drink-soaked howl that went tearing through the paper walls and pierced the dark night outside, awakening most of the dwellers of Shanty Land. Some came out of their huts and called from compound to compound wanting to know what the hell was going on in the village.

'It is the Razor's hut,' someone said.

'Is it on fire?' another asked in the darkness.

'I wish it were. I can't see any though.'

'What in the heavens are they up to?'

'Would you like to go and ask them yourself?'

'Hell. No.'

Doors banged shut.

'Swines,' somebody said in a hushed voice and another door banged shut.

Later, most villagers agreed that they had never had such a night in their ten or more years in Shanty Land.

At the Razor's hut, a small candle burned slowly late into the night and slowly too the fanfare died down to a drunken drone. The Crasher had fallen asleep on the floor after crying his one eye dry. They let him be. Nobody took the trouble to know who had filled the bottle with urine after its contents were exhausted, or even whether he was trying to invent some sort of a cocktail in good faith. Everybody was glad the inventive soul had provided the highlight for the evening. It was very likely that it was the Professor who had had the stroke of genius: the bottle was discovered right next to his sleeping form and nobody remembered seeing him go out to relieve himself when the others had done so. Now however, the whole gang sat back, the episode all but forgotten. Everybody sat around exhausted and feeling it.

'Maina,' the Razor called from his kingly bed.

Maina grunted something resembling an answer.

'Do you know what happened to Kimaitho?' the other asked.

'He drank urine,' Maina said from the depths of drunkenness.

The Razor laughed lightly.

'Leave the Crasher alone,' he said. 'He has only one eye like a motor-cycle and he never went to school so you can't blame him.'

Maina sniggered, his humour aroused.

'Talking of school,' he said. 'Have you ever wondered who trains the cooks in boarding schools?'

'Boarding schools?' somebody asked drunkenly. 'What is that, it sounds familiar.'

'You mean you don't know what that is?' Maina asked and belched. 'Did you desert school early in nursery school?'

'He doesn't even know what that is,' the Razor excused his follower's ignorance. 'He never went to one.'

'And have you?' the ignorant one asked.

The Razor laughed.

'I have more than gone to a nursery school, private,' he said. 'I was learning with Maina in Standard One.'

'What is that?' the other one asked.

The Razor laughed drunkenly.

'Ignorant pig,' he said. 'Tell them about school, Maina. Tell them what we did.'

Maina sighed and hiccuped.

'We sang and played and counted fingers,' he said.

'Was that all?' the Sweeper asked.

Maina looked at him and tried to focus him.

'Yes,' he said.

'No . . . no,' the Razor said. 'Tell them what else you and me did besides counting fingers.'

Maina thought hard. Sleep and tiredness and drunkenness clouded his brain. He hiccuped again.

'Tell them,' the Razor encouraged.

Maina scratched his head.

'We . . . we . . . counted our toes . . . hic . . . hic . . . as well,' he reported.

The Razor grunted.

'You don't remember anything else more interesting?' he asked. 'Don't you remember what you and me and Kimaitho did? We got punished for it remember?'

Maina's head whirled.

'We counted each other's toes and drank urine,' he said drunkenly and belched loudly.

The Razor like the rest of the gang gave up trying to make sense out of Maina's talk. He turned over and faced Sara who was fast asleep by his side.

'You are a swine, Maina,' he told the other sleepily. 'You are my classmate and a swine. Don't you remember how we stole the teacher's bag and ran away from school?'

'I never ran away from any school,' Maina protested. 'I hung on to the bitter end.'

'You are an ass too,' the Razor told him. 'You are a drunken ass.'

Maina laughed uncomprehendingly. All the others in the hut were now asleep and he was drowsy. The candle on the empty bottle had burned its last drop of wax and the tiny flame danced desperately above the bottle. Maina sniggered again as pictures formed, twisted and dissolved in his befuddled head.

'You know Razor,' he said. 'I don't think I ever went with you to school. I don't think you have ever been to school at all. No classmate of mine would snatch bags and run away from school.' He paused to belch again. 'I have read, Razor. I have read many books. I have been to boarding schools and eaten their swirl devotedly and slept on their sacks. I have also sat exams and tried to get a respectable job and slept in bins . . . and . . . and . . . hic . . . worked in dirty little kitchens and joined your mucky gang.'

He paused. The Razor snored in his sleep loudly.

'I also had a friend,' he went on. 'Better friend than you lot ever

69

set your eyes on. And a real earthworm he was too. That boy could turn dirt better than a mole. He was a good boy and I read with him. We went through more books than you monkeys will ever see in your life. I wish Meja were here. He would tell you what I think you people are.'

He hiccuped and swayed sleepily.

'Hear me Razor,' he went on, less strongly than before, sleep weighing down on him. 'You are wasting your time, Razor. You are wasting your time hiding in this little hole, drinking urine and eating insects like a lot of little mice. You are all bastards, Razor. You are all bastards and I like you. I should have . . .'

The candle flame danced desperately in fear of the encroaching darkness. Then with one last struggle as of a dying man, it flickered for the last time and was swallowed in the cold dark. And the whole of Shanty Land was now covered in a curtain of darkness to cover its misery, its happiness, its affections and its secret fears.

Maina dragged himself slowly along the suburban lanes. His patrolling day was over and he was heading home to present his report to the leader of the gang. It had been a very successful day and his friends would no doubt be delighted to hear that soon, very soon they would be eating again. He was fully trained now and he went around alone quite unafraid. He had learned to tolerate policemen as well as he had learned to get on with the Crasher and his band. Policemen were an essential part in the game of life and one could get along with them well enough as long as one gave them no reason to know one's name. One could make good companions of policemen if one kept the hell out of their beat areas. But if one got too friendly, a man might find himself sharing such a privilege as a ride in a patrol car all the way to the station. And there in a dark room a one-sided conversation might well lead to a scholarship to prison.

Against this last atrocity there was only one sensible defence; never try to reason with a policeman in uniform. Once out to earn himself a medal, a policeman could conceive no reasonable possibility that one might be innocent. If you looked innocent, you were hiding something. Many an innocent citizen ended up so confused by his own attempts to prove himself guiltless that he ended up in prison nevertheless. To guard against ever having to go to prison, Maina had one secret rule: *if ever a policeman in uniform who seems to have a vacant place on his chest walks up to you and says, 'hello', turn right round and run as fast as you can and hope he does not catch you.*

How could you possibly explain to him why you are dressed in rags or why you have no shoes on? A policeman could ask you anything, from what you ate for lunch to where you think you will be in December next year. How could you explain why you were standing at the show case and staring at the cake display within so eagerly? If you told him that you had tasted cake once in your lifetime in a farm twenty miles from the city he would then want to know why you were still not at the farm eating cake. He would also want to know what you are doing walking the streets when everybody else is at work. And how could you explain to him that you too were at work minding other peoples pockets for them?

So whichever way you looked at it, you ended up in the can, and the lovable public servant received his beautiful shiny medal and a heavier pay packet. And that was the way to live.

Maina came to the rise leading down to Shanty Land. He stopped and stood there deep in thought. A few ghostly people passed by him and darted little respectful glances in his direction. They knew him already. He was one of the Razor boys; the kinder one who sported a black beard and talked to everybody freely, and whose eyes were not as blank and devoid of love and care as the others. He was the one that did not kick hens and chairs out of his way, and did not spank little children when they accidentally ran into his legs. He was that one who was rarely seen drunk and even then never passed water against the paper walls of other peoples huts or shouted obscene names at his neighbours. It was a remarkable thing that now among the Razors there was one who greeted people with respect and sympathised with them in their problems. On one or two occasions, Maina had lent out money to some citizens who had promised to pay back, though he knew they never could.

Now Maina stood at the top of the rise that led down to his home, and thought. Smoke, dust and the usual hum of life hovered in the air. And the people that passed him on their way back home from their endless search for the means of existence were people he felt that he liked. Given time, he felt he might even come to love them. He compared the citizens of Shanty Land with the farm hands on Boi's farm. On the farm, the men had been completely subdued, resigned to being led around by a fat white man and a monster of a foreman. It seemed they lived only for the halved ration of flour and bottle of skimmed milk.

In Shanty Land, people were on the move. True, they did not have much, but then there was no boss and no foreman to shove them in any direction. Everybody was boss in his own little hut. Everybody went about feeding his own family. And everybody was looking forward to a future of some sort. Often you could hear a Shanty Land veteran who had been there for ages and who was now accelerating towards the grave, say 'When I get money, I will . . .' And that was the right spirit in which to go about life. Maina knew it was the right spirit for it was the same sort of hope that had carried him through school, the backstreets and the farm, to where he now stood, the heavenly free Shanty Land.

'Hello,' someone said behind Maina.

He spun round quickly. Then he relaxed.

'Hello, Delilah,' he said thrusting his hand out to her.

The girl, one of the most beautiful young maidens in Shanty Land, looked him up and down.

'You are worried,' she told him.

He shook his head and smiled.

'I am thinking,' he corrected.

'About?'

'About you, my dear, who else would it be,' he told her.

She smiled back.

'Well?' she said.

'Where have you been?' he asked her.

She stood looking up at him for a moment. Large black eyes, long black eyelashes, a small round face and smiling lips that revealed a row of evenly trimmed teeth just beginning to turn brown at the tips.

'I have been at work,' she answered.

'You work?' Maina was surprised.

'Yes,' she smiled.

The smile was a challenge to Maina. She could work and she was working.

'Since when?'

'Three days now.'

Maina smiled, squeezed her little hand and looked right into her eyes.

'Where?'

'In town.'

'Town?'

'In the Friends Bar.'

Maina raised his eyebrows.

'Barmaid,' she told him.

And Maina now had need to hold on to his smile. He shook his head and made a crackling little noise with his mouth. It was with this gesture that he had captivated her a few months back.

She shook her head and opened her eyes wide.

'You don't like it?' she asked.

Maina tried to cover up his confusion by patting her shoulder and squeezing her hand harder. But she caught him out and he knew she knew why he was afraid. He tried to smile and ended up grinning hideously.

'I won't leave you, Maina,' she said urgently.

Maina laughed foolishly.

'Never?'

'Never.'

He laughed again.

'Not even if I am a thief and a robber and a drunkard, and . . . and jobless.'

'Not even if you are the most crooked, one-eyed, one-legged devil in the world.'

Maina smiled, shook his head and started to make the crackling sound but before he could do it, Delilah pursed her lips and made the noise for him.

They both laughed nervously and she moved closer to stare up at his face. He squeezed her shoulders and started to kiss her forehead. Somebody coughed behind them. They sprang apart and Maina looked over his shoulder. An old woman passed behind them smiling that I-know smile and hobbled down to Shanty Land. Delilah disengaged herself.

'I must be going now,' she said.

'Why the great hurry,' he asked her. 'Are you ashamed of being seen with me then?'

'You shouldn't say that,' she told him. 'You know what I feel about you. But sometimes I wonder about you. You act so . . . so funny.'

Maina took hold of her hands and looked down into her hurt face.

'You know I like you,' he told her.

'Well?' she said. 'Only that?'

'And not a little.'

'You like me very much?'

'A bit more.'

'You like me very, very much?'

'Yes,' Maina told her. 'Very, very much and then some more.'

'You love me?' she smiled broadly.

Maina smiled with her and tried to hide his fears.

'Maina, will you marry me?' she asked slipping her hands behind his back.

The question hit him like a sledge hammer but he smiled boldly.

'When?' he asked her.

She thought hard.

'That is a good question,' she agreed. 'When will you marry me, Maina?'

Maina smiled again but his head was hot with the conflict within.

'I asked you the question,' he told her. 'You tell me the answer.'

She cocked her head to look up at his eyes.

'Won't anything come out of this?' she asked, suddenly serious.

73

Maina shrugged helplessly.

'I wonder,' she said. 'I very much wonder.'

'So do I,' Maina said almost to himself.

'You know I love you, Maina?' she said.

'Sure,' he said.

The real truth was that he too loved her. She was the only person in the whole of Shanty Land and the only woman in the world who really understood his every emotion, his every problem and most of all, his fears. But he did not want to admit to her there and then that he loved her. She should have guessed that too. He would have liked to marry her. But he just could not do so and he did not want to hurt her trying to explain. That nothing more than good company would come out of their friendship was no secret. She ought to have known. It was as obvious as the fact that he loved her. But then women always did put affection before reasoning.

'You haven't answered my question, Maina,' she told him. 'Will you . . .'

'Can't we . . . just love and be friends without having to go that far?' he asked her.

'You don't understand,' she told him. 'A girl wants to be loved and married and children and . . . You just can't understand.'

'I understand,' Maina told her.

He understood only too well. He had heard that before, long ago during his school days. That time he had been trapped into foolishly promising a lot of things. A lot of things that never materialised. And now he knew better. He was older and wiser. He understood everything. A woman wanted to be loved, yes. But she also wanted some more. She wanted a husband, a home, children and happiness and security. Apart from love Maina had nothing else to offer. He could not take her into the Razor's hut as his wife; no there were enough troubles in there already without adding more. Sara would not stand for another female in the harem, and nor would the Razor. And what would they do with children in the gang? Children needed to be brought up by a father who could keep them satisfied seven days a week, twenty-four hours a day. Maina could not promise anything of the sort. He himself did not eat seven days a week, even one meal a day. If Delilah wanted marriage, he would have to leave her, for her own sake, to another man who could provide her with at least a home and some security. It would hurt him, he knew, but it had to be done. Yes, love was not exactly all that really mattered.

'I must go now,' she said and disentangled herself from his arms.

'I would like to see you again,' he told her.

'I will be on duty tonight,' she said with tears in her voice.

'At the bar?'

'You don't seem to like it.'

'I don't like to see you seeing other men,' he said.

'I would gladly serve you,' she said

He jerked away and she realised that she had insulted him. She busied herself with her hands, but a tear or two rolled down her cheeks. Her man could never be a real man, he could never sit high on a bar stool and make jokes at her and get sodden drunk and be a real man. He knew this too.

'When do I see you next then?' he asked. 'Tomorrow night?'

She looked down and thought.

'Yes, tomorrow night,' she said.

'See you then,' Maina grunted.

He stood watching her go, swinging her large hips. Beneath the blue dress her plump body looked very enticing. Maina scratched his head and shook it. Then he marched down to Shanty Land, taking quick short steps and whistling an old pop song that was suddenly full of new meaning. The song, he remembered was called 'Somewhere My Love'.

The gang was in, sober and hungry and as gloomy as ever. When there was no Nubian Gin and no food and bhang, absent also were fun and laughter, song and life. This was the Razor's gang. Maina tried to picture what they had been before they became crooks and bhang addicts. He saw them as small boys running about in some village with their shirts flying like banners behind and no shorts on at all. Their bodies were coarse and hard like the skin of some mud-burrowing creature. Their hair was a zoo for lice and bugs. Washing caused a riot in the home, and everybody knew that they were taking a bath from the kind of racket that they caused. The only peaceful bath they ever had was an accidental splash as their mothers were throwing out a bucketful of dirty water. To them tooth-pulling was a revolution and a whole army of neighbours had to be called in to reinforce mother as she pulled out the old tooth to make way for the new one. Maina had gone through the same line of evolution so he knew all about them and understood them well.

When Maina came into the hut the gang were lying in an assortment of weird positions. They only showed that they were alive by occasionally opening their eyes and finding a better position for their bottoms. The Razor lay on his bed, alone. All he did was turn his head to see who had entered the hut.

'Anything?' he enquired.

'A lot,' Maina said and threw himself on a crate in the corner of the hut and looked around.

There were a few visitors in the room – a fireplace, two cooking pots, a number of tin plates and some tin mugs and spoons. These had come to visit a few months back when Maina, single handed, raided a house in stark daylight, and while the owner was in, and made off with a coat full of money. The coat was now the Razor's kingly cape. Sara in an attack of womanliness had bought the expensive luxuries, but now it was doubtful whether they would last much longer. With financial depression becoming acute and likely to get worse, the utensils were getting further and further from being wanted and nearer to the pawn shop. The fireplace, well, that too would go: it was becoming a nuisance by consuming the crates they used for sitting on. Already one of the bars in the roof had disappeared in its hungry flames. Somebody would soon have to go some place for firewood and no one in the gang had the necessary energy to spare. The fireplace would have to go soon. Maina's face twisted into a smile.

The Razor watched him quietly.

'What did you get?' he asked.

'Nothing today,' Maina said.

Those in the gang who had bothered to open their eyes closed them again at this announcement. Somebody's stomach rumbled a protest.

'Tomorrow?' the Razor asked.

'Not even the day after,' Maina told him. 'It will take days and a lot of patience. It might also involve, ah,' he paused significantly, 'a little cash.'

The Razor turned his head to look at the paper wall.

'What for?' he enquired.

Maina looked at the form on the bed, shrugged and looked away.

'I shall require a file, some paper and a pen,' he said.

'Huh?' the Razor faced him again with interest this time.

'Yes,' Maina told him. 'This time I will try something different. Something new. This time I will use paper and pen like I was taught to do.'

The Razor stared up at the sooty roof of the hut.

'Forgery?' he asked.

Maina shook his head.

'Nothing that primitive,' he said. 'It's something modern. Something totally new. Something which, if it comes off, will pay a hundred, two hundred times what it costs. It is great.'

The Razor sighed.

'It had better be,' he said. 'We cannot afford to waste time and money on something small.'

'I shall also require a white overall,' Maina said.

The Razor twisted his neck to stare at the other man, rolled on to his stomach and put his head in his hands.

Outside, shanty life hummed on as though the Razor's hut and its load of troubles did not exist. And inside the hut, the gang idled, weighed down by their hungers and hopelessness.

'And what is this big deal of yours?' the Razor demanded.

Maina smiled slyly.

'It is like this . . .'

6

MAINA WOKE UP very early. He had a few things to straighten out before the plan got under way. The other gang members were still asleep when he left Shanty Land and headed out to where his business lay. A few cars passed him along the roads and once he had to dive into a trench to avoid the keen eyes of the occupants of a prowling patrol car. Street lamps were just beginning to go out. In Cedar Avenue he marked all the houses where watch dogs raced to the gates of houses to bark at him. He marked also the best approach to each house. Finished with Cedar Avenue he turned down a by-way and was soon in Eastern Retreat. There under the sheltering gloom of a large tree he stopped and waited.

The milkman came down Eastern Retreat and Maina fell in a few houses behind him. The man stopped at every house to deposit a pint or two of milk and then moved on whistling. Maina noted every move. They turned west to Western Close and followed the same procedure. At the end of the Close the dairy truck was waiting for the lone milkman. The milkman got in beside the driver and Maina lay flat in a ditch to avoid being caught in the headlights as the truck accelerated out of the Close to deliver its milk to another part of the suburbs. When the tail-lights vanished, the petrol fumes still hanging in the atmosphere, Maina got to his feet. He hastened out of the danger area in the direction of the safety of Shanty Land.

He heard the noise when he was about half a mile from home. It was a low rumbling sound, punctuated by a sharp crackling like that of breaking dry sticks. Looking over the low houses towards Shanty Land, he saw a thick black cloud of smoke rising slowly to the skies, accompanied by galaxies of sparks and tongues of giant flames. Then came the tinkling bell of a fire-engine, and a fire siren.

His heart thumping and his head numb, he started running. He ran, tripped and fell and ran again towards his home. It took him but a short time to get to the top of the rise that overlooked the valley. His body was hot and his chest sore. Sweat poured from him and his clothes stuck to his body.

At the top of the rise he came upon the whole populace of Shanty Land. They were standing together in the gloom like frightened cattle, their meagre belongings collected in bundles around them. Here and there, a child cried at being awakened at such an early hour. The women soothed the children while the men dived in and out of the flames to try and save precious possessions. The flames roared into a crescendo now and illuminated the frightened faces. Some of the women and most of the children were half naked and the men were in under-pants and vests straight from bed, sweat glistening on their bony shoulders as they fought the impoverishing flames.

A few huts at the edge of Shanty Land were as yet untouched and these the fire-men battled to save. But it was a losing battle as the fire spread amongst the huts, roaring its hunger for destruction. A citizen loaded with belongings emerged from the flames, his eyes set wide, his tongue sticking out as though in thirst. As the crowd stared, a baby started screaming as the mother swooned into her collection of crockery and crate furniture.

Two bulky firemen disengaged themselves from the task of hacking down huts and searching for survivors. They sprinted to the collapsed man and lifting him from amongst his collection of cooking pans and rags bore him to the top of the rise where first-aid people were at work tending people suffering from shock, minor scratches and burns. The wealth the man had risked his life to save was left where he had fallen, and the flames had an easy job reducing it to a heap of useless grey ash.

There was no piped water anywhere near the shacks, and the fire-men, after saving what they could, stepped back to watch the flames lick what they could not save. Then in a hut close to the edge of the burning village, the cry of a hurt child rang through the flames. A fireman started towards the hut and had taken only three steps when the roof collapsed in a fresh cloud of dark ugly smoke. The cries of the child were drowned in the ensuing flames. The fireman shielded his face from the heat of the flames and shuffled back defeated. More women fainted.

A fleet of ambulances arrived in a flourish of sirens.

Dawn approached fast.

Maina watched with the others, incapable of any movement and choking with heat, smoke and cries of anguish around him. Grief shook his body sporadically. He thought about his beloved gang. He had left them sound asleep. Were they all right?

The flames roared one last round of anger and malice and sent a hail of giant sparks into the ever lightening sky. Day was coming and the fire had done its work. Its colour changed from crimson red, like fresh blood, to yellow and the flames became shorter. The roar changed to soft mocking laughter as the fire set smugly about finishing the work it had started. The cloud of smoke lessened and small particles of soot started settling down on people's heads, their eyes, their belongings. As the early morning wind sprang up, the smoke was carried away

79

from the valley into the city centre and beyond, spreading its message of sorrow to the suburbs with their beautiful roads and clean lawns.

Maina was searching among the survivors for his friends. The police had arrived and were moving among the people, urging anyone with any information that might lead to the discovery of the cause of the fire to step forward. Crowds of people from other parts of the city too stood at a distance and watched what remained of Shanty Land and its citizens. There was not much of it left worth watching. Why nobody had bothered to come and watch when the village was in full swing, Maina could not understand.

He found the Razor leaning on a tree, a little way from the crowd, with the others sitting faithfully around him. The loyal family could not mix with the ordinary crowd even in a crisis. Maina had never been so glad to see them. His world was centred around these unlearned people, with their confused doctrines, and their brains disordered by drugs, alcohol and misuse of their common sense.

When the sun came up the gang were still staring down on the ruins, talking in nods and shakes and moans. Firemen now started their search for only they knew what: the tell-tale charred little bones which would help list the number of the victims of the fire.

The Razor stood up. The others did the same. The Professor sniffled. They followed the Razor away from the little valley.

'Where are we going?' somebody asked.

'What are we going to do?' the Crasher asked in a defeated tone.

Their questions hung in the air, unanswered.

Razor turned to Maina.

'What happened?' Maina asked.

'We were asleep,' the Razor said and no more.

Maina sighed.

'You did your patrolling all right?' the Razor asked.

Maina nodded.

'When do you start?' the Razor asked him.

'Tomorrow morning,' Maina answered. 'Is everything ready?'

The Razor handed him a bundle he had been carrying under his arm. He weighed it with his hands.

'Is this everything?'

'Everything.'

They walked in silence for some time, still following the Razor. It was his responsibility as the leader to lead them to a place of safety and he knew it. And even Sara kept quiet, trusting in his wisdom. The sun rose higher and was hot. They passed through the suburbs, a party of ragged misery and loss. Then they headed for the outskirts of the city. The gang was becoming weary when Maina could stand the silence no longer and he posed the all-important questions.

'Where are we going,' he asked. 'What are we going to do?'

They were now walking in formation, the Razor, Sara and Maina in the front, while the rest followed in threes.

The Razor answered Maina's questions without turning.

'We must start again,' he said. 'I know a place outside the city. It is a good place. We have to live. We are going to do just that.'

His mind whirled round. Somewhere in a dark forested valley, he knew a place. There flowed a sweet water spring and on the banks of it, life would start all over again. There among the dark cool shadows of the forest Shanty Land would be reborn. And just as they had done before, the other citizens of Shanty Land would follow him to this new land. More paper, tin and mud huts would go up and within a night Shanty Land would be alive again. They would all come. He knew it. There was nowhere else to go. Like frightened animals hunted by fear and poverty, they would seek refuge among the trees with him. To the Razor, Shanty Land was not dead, turned to ashes by a mysterious sea of fire. It had merely fallen asleep and would arise again soon, in another valley, next to a lonely stream. All it took was some paper, a little old tin, some mud and a little will. Yes, the will to live.

7

THE OCCUPANTS of Cedar Avenue had had problems with their milk for a long time. None of the city dairies, it seemed, was ready any longer to risk its money and time driving milk-trucks along the narrow avenue so full of ruts that milk bottles broke as the lorry jolted along. At one time, to cover any damage caused by the bad avenue, especially when the rains came and the trucks skidded into overflowing ditches, the dairies had charged the milk consumers a few extra cents; but they then complained that the people of the area turned out to be thieves, likely to take off to God-knows-where leaving the milk bills unmet. That was the atmosphere between the dairies and the dwellers of Cedar Avenue. Local citizens had to buy their milk from the city and save it for a whole day, while those of the neighbouring roads received their milk punctually every morning.

Thus the wives of the 'thieves' of Cedar Avenue were more than surprised when one afternoon a milkman with a long black beard and blood-shot eyes walked the entire length of the avenue to tell them that a new dairy in the city was ready to start delivering milk to them daily, good weather or foul. This caused a cheer to rise from the milk-loving housewives. And the conditions were simple too. Any good citizen had only to pay an advance of fifty per cent of the cost of a whole month's milk delivered. Consultations were held during the late hours of the night between the 'thieves' of Cedar Avenue and their wives. Husbands grunted, wives cooed and the deal was settled. Most of the husbands agreed that although they were hard pressed financially, they could afford at least the advance money. Nobody mentioned anything about meeting the rest of the bill at the end of the month. Wives giggled and fell asleep assured that in future there would be enough milk to drink and swim in.

The following day, Maina walked down Cedar Avenue dressed in milkman's white overall and carrying a file in one hand and a ballpoint pen behind his ear. His hair was combed and his boots polished clumsily with borrowed black polish plus a little powdered coal. He walked from house to house collecting money and entering the name of the subscriber and the number of his house into his file. He did not speak much for fear of confusing questions. A few housewives mistook his fear for shyness and against their husbands' orders decided to be nice to the shy young man and paid him the full one month's money. On such an occasion Maina smiled really shyly.

'Thank you very much, madam,' he said. 'You will get your milk very early tomorrow morning.'

Then he walked to the next house in the line. Maina knew just how to deal with these suburban women. From the time he had worked for them chopping wood and cleaning lawns, he had come to know that one could not afford to reason with a woman of the suburbs. As soon as one became reasonable, the woman would take offence and fly off to the interior of the house where no one, let alone a milkman, dared follow. So he handled them softly the way they liked and gave way where he had to.

All in all Maina netted five pounds from the stingy occupants of Cedar Avenue. This was more than he had hoped for and he told himself his scheme was coming on very well. If only he could stick the game long enough.

When he returned tired to new Shanty Town that evening there were the usual rowdy celebrations and merry-making. And everybody felt extra warm towards Maina for his initiative. Sara also could not hide her feelings for him and she hugged and kissed him in front of the Razor's disapproving eyes. Self-preservation told Maina to discourage the girl from ever repeating such an insult to her man; but the rest, Sweeper, Crasher, Professor and all, were too busy living for the moment to notice the warning glance.

'Eat and drink, my friends,' Maina invited them. 'Tomorrow I am in real business.'

Then Professor had an attack of kindness and offered to go with him and be useful.

'No ... no,' Maina said seriously. 'This is new business. Real business. Respectable business. It needs personality and intelligence, two things I am sure you have never heard of. You would only mess up things. No my son,' he shook his head and belched loudly. 'You stay right here and eat and try to grow up here,' he pointed at his head. 'Papa Maina will work for you.'

They drank to the success of Papa Maina's new venture and then to the rapid growth of Professor's brain. And later that night, very late, they went to sleep, fed, drunk and tired. Their hearts were contented and it was almost like old Shanty Land.

Maina woke up earlier than usual. Working people did not sleep late and he was not going to be the exception. He went down to the stream, washed his face and wet his rough beard. Back at the hut he donned his white overalls and started for the suburbs. His file of names, numbers and quantities of milk wanted was folded and neatly tucked under his armpit. In his other hand he carried a large basket, mysteriously procured by the Sweeper.

He was waiting at the end of Eastern Retreat when the usual milkman came round, walking with the usual leisurely gait and whistling the usual busy song. Maina fell in behind him, but a safe distance behind. And every time a bottle of milk was placed outside a dark closed door he picked it up and placed it tenderly in his basket. The other milkman went busily about his business and so did Maina. Eastern Retreat finished with, they walked down to Western Close and the same procedure was repeated. Milk bottles diminished in the milkman's basket and increased in Maina's. At the end of the Close, Maina once more dived into the ditch while the milk truck carried the dairyman away. He then retrieved the last bottles and headed breathlessly back the way he had come.

Back to his own territory he deposited the bottles from door to door, where no milk had been placed for months. His duty done, he folded his basket into a bundle and hid it inside a cedar bush. Then he fled back to new Shanty Land and his friends to await developments.

That day the occupants of Cedar Avenue had sweet white milk, enough to drink and swim in, while those of the Retreat and the Close had black tea for breakfast and the husbands had to make an emergency call back home in the middle of the morning to make sure the baby had his customary feed. They thought something had gone wrong with the milk truck although most of them could have sworn they had heard its rattle and the milkman's whistle that morning. They hoped they would find a double share the following morning and an apology note from the dairy. But for one week running there was neither apology note nor milk for Eastern Retreat and Western Close. While the housewives of Cedar Avenue enjoyed their milk every morning and some husbands were even thinking of putting milk money into their monthly budget.

Protesting phone calls started flowing into the desk of the directing manager of the Central Dairies. They were all from Eastern Retreat and Western Close and they were all complaining about the missing milk. The manager could make neither head nor tail of the whole thing so he called in the clerk. They put their heads together, murmured for a few minutes and decided that three heads were better than two. So they called in the foreman. The three put their heads together and decided to call the truck driver and try four heads. The driver swore the milk had been delivered punctually every morning. He also swore that he had not driven the milk to the wrong street by mistake. He was positive about that. But milk in glass bottles could not evaporate just like that. Not together with the bottles anyway.

Cats and homeless mongrels came into the question too, but no one had heard of a cat or a dog that could drink milk and eat the bottles as well. Quick phone calls were made and it was ascertained that no sign of broken bottles had been seen outside any of the houses in the affected areas.

The milkman concerned was called in and made to swear that he had delivered the milk every morning to the complainants' doors. That set the Central Dairies Board of Directors thinking and for a full day they sat and argued and exchanged bitter words. They had reached the point of accusing one another of subversive activities when reason walked in. For the hundredth time they put their heads together and this time they did not fly apart. With sweating brows they came up with an answer. Behind the whole thing they saw a diabolical plan by the honourable citizens of the Eastern Retreat and the Western Close. Purpose of the plan: to get a free one week's supply of pure full cream, fresh, white milk. This made the directors furious.

An S.O.S. was sent to the Central Police Station. The most brilliant of all brilliant detectives went round to the offices of the Central Dairies. Questions were asked and notes made. Nobody liked the way the detectives asked their questions, least of all the milkman himself. He thought the detectives asked questions as though they suspected him of drinking up all the milk entrusted to him to deliver to the consumers.

Back at the police station meetings were held, and then the detectives drove to the two affected streets to question the complainants. One of the police detectives actually lived in this area and so he knew how it was to be without fresh milk for one full week. Notes were again compared at the station, and before long the detectives too put two and two together. They found that their answer to the problem was a rotten public nuisance known in the common language as a thief. But what would anyone with one mouth and one stomach want so much milk for?

The relevant orders were issued forthwith. Heels clicked and hands were raised in salute.

It was early Monday morning. A light drizzle was falling and fog and mist hung ghostly along the suburban streets. A lone figure in a white overall made its way along the dimly lighted street and melted into the darkness close to the fence whenever a patrol car came prowling around, its occupants yawning tiredly and peering into the misty morning with sleepy eyes. The lonely walker then pulled a parcel from the cedar bush, which when straightened out turned out to be a palm leaf basket. He walked down to Cedar Avenue, turned left into Eastern Retreat and hid behind a bush. He did not have long to wait. The milkman came soon after, whistling his usual song and depositing his milk bottles from door to door. The waiting figure followed quietly behind, collecting milk bottles from door to door.

Somewhere along the route, a dark shadow stirred and turned into a mackintoshed phantom. His head was covered by a ferret hat hung low over his face. He waited until the milkman passed and then waited until the milk collector came along panting slightly from the loaded basket. He walked boldly and collected bottles as though there was nothing to it. The dark watcher even thought that he heard the milk collector whistling the same tune that the milkman was whistling as he went about his business. The three went from house to house, from door to door, one unaware of the two, the other unaware of one and the last aware of both the others and their missions.

They turned into Western Close and continued the system as before. The following shadow was then joined by another, also wearing an overcoat and a hat. His hands were thrust deep into his pockets to keep them safe from the cold morning drizzle. They did not speak. They just followed their prey as he too followed his prey. The milk-truck was waiting as usual at the end of the Close and it carried the milkman away.

Maina, quite oblivious of the two shadows following him, retrieved the last bottles and made his way out of the Close. And he was glad for this was the last day of his ordeal. After today he would go to the housewives of Cedar Avenue and claim the other half of the month's milk charges. He was sure they would pay him if he mentioned the rain and the bad condition of the avenue. If that did not work, he would threaten them with stoppage of deliveries unless they paid. They would have to pay him or miss his sweet milk. In any case he was getting tired of waking up so early in the cold morning. He wanted to sleep like the other boys. He would have to vanish without trace before somebody from either the Close or the Retreat alerted his greatest enemies, the police. He had counted on one week and that was now over, it was time to drop out of sight before somebody caught on to him. After today the Cedar Avenue occupants could milk their chickens if they had any, or even their . . .

He came to the first house and left the first bottle. The golden droplets of drizzle were illuminated by the fading sodium street lamps. He shielded his eyes from the rain and made his way carefully along the puddle-covered avenue. Occasionally a dog barked at him, but he was not alarmed. He had made sure not to register any dog-owning family for his charity milk delivery. Dogs could be nasty in the gloomy hours of the morning.

Maina was cold and wet but his heart was full of song. His task was nearing completion. He hummed the popular 'Freedom Train' soul number and remembered Delilah, sweet plump little Delilah. She had not come with the rest of the crowd to new Shanty Land and Maina sometimes wondered where she might have gone. He missed her terribly at times and he would soon go back to old Shanty Land to try and trace her. Maina was feeling so flamboyant he even kissed the last bottle before setting it down on the last doorstep. His heart was full of freedom and Delilah and another song, 'Cold Sweat', came to his lips. He was beginning to whistle the tune when he turned to go.

He froze in his steps even as the song did on his lips. Real cold sweat broke all over his skin and mingled with the damp left by the drizzle. His muscles slowly contracted as his eyes darted this way and that looking for a getaway. There was none. The two black-coated men blocked the only way out of the verandah. The game was up.

'Hello,' one of the men said.

Hemmed in the way he was by the verandah and the two blocking his only way out, Maina had no choice but to play the game the way they wanted, or get hurt. Already he could guess who they were. He thought quickly. A bluff might do if they did not know what he was up to. But the big question was: just for how long had they been following him?

'Hello,' he said innocently. 'Central Dairy, can I help you?'

One of the two men laughed.

'Hear that, Inspector?' the man said to the other. 'This boy has got nerves.'

'I am not surprised,' the other said. 'He would need them to do what he has been doing.'

'Put your hands up,' the first man commanded.

His hand held a black little thing that looked like a gun. His companion stood with his hands still deep in his pockets. The two men's eyes bored into Maina paralysing him with fear of what might happen if he did not obey their orders, and in the background his old fear of prisons. His hands rose mechanically. They kept rising until they could go no further without tearing out their sockets.

The unarmed man took his hands from his pockets with a packet of cigarettes and a lighter. He selected a cigarette without looking at it and stuck it in the corner of his mouth. He lighted it and put the lighter and the packet back into his pocket. Then he regarded Maina with curious interest.

'Maybe you can tell me what you are doing?' he asked Maina coldly.

Maina trembled at the voice. He tried to say something and failed the pronunciation.

'Or maybe you will speak better at the station,' the other man told him. 'Pick up that bottle and let us go find out.'

Maina hesitated.

'Pick up that bottle,' the man ordered.

Maina's hands came down and his back bent for the bottle. At the apparent domicility of their captive the armed detective put his pistol back into his pocket; but as Maina's back straightened, his will to live and love of freedom reasserted themselves. His back snapped back and the milk bottle flew from his grasp.

'Watch!' the smoking policeman shouted as the missile came at them.

They side-stepped simultaneously and the bottle smashed uselessly on the stone footpath. Maina dived, aiming for the only route to freedom – between the startled policemen. But he slipped as he left the verandah and went crashing into the waiting arms of the law. Handcuffs clicked. Then his captors set about showing him how not to treat two detective inspectors on night duty.

Maina's head and body were aching from the beating when at last a patrol car pulled up and he was hauled in. The other bottles were all collected. Just as the street lamps flickered off, a police patrol car headed away from the suburbs, a handcuffed milk-thief between two satisfied detectives in the back seat.

8

THE LARGE ORANGE BUS with a blue streak across its middle laboured along the dusty road leading to Ngaini Village. It was laden with heavy loads of bananas, yams, and other farm produce for this was market day. It also carried a load of tired men and women. The huge wheels of the vehicle bit into the dust, slipped and bit again and the old engine roared to its last measure of power and pushed the bus and its load another few inches forward. The driver bit his lower lip and wrestled with the steering wheel, his cap tilting at an angle on his head. But the crowd in the bus neither recognised the driver's efforts nor the old machine's. All they cared was that they got home in time for milking the cows. Some were still arguing with the conductor as to how much money they should be charged for their luggage. And when they opened their mouths to speak they emitted a foul stench of unwashed mouths and tobacco.

Inconspicuously in the corner of the back seat sat a young man with tattered clothes and a bewildered face. His large eyes flitted miserably here and there, from one face to the next, and dropped at once whenever any of the faces glanced back. Every now and then the young man's nose twisted at the smell of sweaty bodies, tobacco and ripe bananas. The noise in the bus was deafening as every passenger raised his voice in order to be heard above the rattle, and this in turn only increased the noise so that none could hear what the other was saying. But the passengers went right on retelling the day's occurrences at the market regardless of whether they were understood or not. And in the corner of the bus the young man watched with a twitching nose and drew comfort from the fact that these were his people, that they spoke his merry tongue, and he could understand. Nobody asked him what he was doing there in the corner or where he was going and he was glad about this too.

The bus swam in a sea of dust and exhaust smoke as with its one eye it sought or felt its way around the familiar countryside. The eyes of the young man missed nothing as he looked out of the tiny window which was no larger than an open exercise book. Here and there, he saw a landmark that he remembered. These familiar marks from the past stirred up memories in his mind and he sat and let the memories come and go as they wished.

D 89

Banana plantations floated mysteriously by the window of the bus and the wind was distinctly heard whispering on the enormous green expanse of leaves. Maize plantations also came and went and occasionally a woman was seen bent to her exhausting task of clearing space for the plants among the weeds. The eyes of the young man saw all this and he wondered. Banana plants trying to exist together on the crowded plot of land, maize plants trying to keep growing in spite of the efforts of the hungry weeds to stop them, and the old woman trying to make a living withal. This perpetual fight for existence had been going on for as long as the young man could remember, only he had never taken note of it before. It had not meant a thing to him until he joined in the struggle. And now it seemed all so real. So painfully real. The noise in the bus receded to the back of his mind to make room for his new line of thought and he wondered even more.

The old bus came to the centre of the village and lurched to a stop. The driver took off his cap, mopped at his brow and let out a sigh of relief. He had made it again in spite of the odds. The market-goers hopped out and started shouting directions to the conductors who were busy unloading the bus. Those whose relatives had come to meet them shook hands with them and talked excitedly. The noise rose to market level.

The young man lingered in the back seat of the bus, his heart pounding and sweat pouring down his face. His stomach contracted painfully and he was short of breath. But he had to get out of the bus and go home, he kept telling himself, although his very soul was revolted against the idea. It had all been easy, thinking of coming back home when he was out in the city, hungry, lost and in pain. It had all been a good idea then, but now! Now it seemed like the worst nightmare he had ever had. Having to go home after so many years of hopelessness and nothing to show for it! Nothing but scars of misery and rough living.

Slowly with great effort, he came to his feet and stretched his dull muscles. He looked down at his torn clothes and passed his hand over his shaven head. Then with a slight limp of his right leg he crept out of the bus and into the cold late afternoon air. Most of the villagers who had come in the bus had dispersed to their homes and those who remained were desperately trying to solve the problem of confused possessions. The young man passed behind them, his heart still beating a painful rhythm in his thin rib cage and his stomach contracted so much with fear that he walked almost doubled up. He did not now care to dry off the sweat that threatened to drown his eyes and face. The last thing he wanted was to be noticed by anyone. Of all things he hated strangers and their harsh questions. Unfortunately he caught the attention of an old woman who was desperately in need of help.

'Here, young man,' she told him. 'Help me move this load.'

The young man hesitated. Then seeing the expecting, almost commanding look on the woman's face, he consented. Struggling with his lame hand, which he tried to hide as much as he could, he helped her move her big load. The old woman was not satisfied however, and she made him help move another load; then she got hold of his hand and led him back to the bus.

'Stay here, young man,' she told him. 'You have more work to help me at.'

The woman started giving directions to the conductors off-loading the bus.

'There is a bunch of bananas somewhere up there,' she said. 'Get it down quick.'

The two conductors on top looked at one another and made faces.

'Quickly,' she shouted, fearing that the young carrier might go away before helping her move that one too.

'But,' one of the conductors said, 'which bunch of bananas?'

The woman made a disgusted shriek.

'A green bunch of bananas,' she cried. 'Bring it down. Quick.'

The conductors looked at one another again. The one who had not spoken turned to look down on the woman.

'All bunches of bananas are green up here,' he told her. 'And they are many.'

The old woman nearly flew into hysterics.

'It is up there,' she screamed. 'You put it up there. If you have lost it . . .'

'How is your bunch of bananas?' the other conductor interposed. 'Is it the big green bunch of bananas, or the bigger greener bunch of bananas or is it the biggest greenest bunch of . . .'

The woman screamed her wrath at them.

'Throw my bananas down you worthless . . .'

The two conductors shrugged simultaneously. Then they started working and bananas literally rained down on the waiting people. Bunches broke apart in mid-air and flew in different directions. A cry of protest rose from the owners. Bananas finished with, boxes and bags and chairs and tables followed. Those who saw them coming clutched at their belongings and sank to the ground under the weight. The conductors were out for fun now. So when the luggage was done with they threw down the ropes and canvasses used for protecting the rack during rainy weather, and a cloud of dust hung in the air. Then they sat down on the rack to watch the problem of large green bananas and larger greener bananas sort itself out. It was at this point, when everybody was looking after their lost luggage, that the young man took the chance to limp away. His head was in a daze and he did not know

91

where he was going, though he felt vaguely that the path he was following was familiar, and that he did not want to go where it went. But his legs kept moving and he limped towards his home.

The sun was about to set and the village and the huts were now a little way behind him. He was in the midst of a maize field, still following the path. The evening wind made a switching sound on the blades of the leaves and this stirred something painful in the young man's consciousness. His head was revolving in the past, way way back in the distant past when he was a little boy and walked along this same path in the evening going to and from the village. The music of the field was sweet then because it spoke of home, home, sweet home, security and satisfaction. Now the noise was hushed and icy cold like the cold of death waiting to spring on him as soon as darkness fell. He quickened his pace, his body trembling and his right leg aching sporadically. And the sun kept on its journey to the west getting dimmer and colder every minute.

He came to the fork in the path. To the right it led to his home and to the left on and on through the neighbours' lands to the wilderness and strangers. Here he stopped and hesitated, one foot on the path that led to his father's house and the other on the other path that led into the distant unknown. His head cried for release from indecision and his body began to tremble. Some invisible barrier blocked the way. Thus he paused and wrestled with his thoughts and fears.

'Meja,' an excited voice called in front of him.

The young man started, nearly collapsed and tried to focus his thoughts on the caller. His heart now shook his whole body with every beat and hot salty sweat stung his eyes. He rubbed them with the back of his scarred hand, and saw her through the mist and fog.

The rays of the setting sun fell on a tiny twelve-year-old girl standing in front of him. She was dressed in a dirty old calico sheet knotted over one shoulder and fastened with a pin below the armpit. The knot was shiny with grime and her collarbone was white beneath the skin. Her head was closely shaven and hard. Her eyes peered at him from the depths of the sockets and a long thread-like neck held the head high above the thin chest. The only thing that showed that the little creature was a girl were the two pimples of breasts that stuck out of her thin chest and showed vaguely under the sheet she wore. Meja watched the pathetic little figure that was his sister and his stomach ached.

He staggered to a fence post and hung on it trying to stop from falling. The little girl run up to him and into his arms. He fell on one knee so that now his face was level with hers. He could not get any word out of his mouth. But the little girl was very happy.

'Meja,' she cried. 'You have come back?'

Meja closed his eyes and opened them again.

'Yes,' he stammered.

The little girl giggled, held his neck tightly with frail little arms and kissed his forehead.

'I am very happy, Meja,' she told him.

Meja groaned something and his head throbbed in rhythm to the sound of distant cow-bells and clinking milking pails. Life was busy all over the land, but where the two stood it was dead. The sound of calves crying for their mothers and the smell of dung and of fields and of home seemed to come from the unwanted past and interfere with the peace of the lonely path.

'Meja,' the girl called.

Meja stammered something.

'You brought me, Meja?' she enquired.

'Brought you?' Meja was wide awake now.

His brain whirled round but he could make no sense out of the question.

'The necklace, Meja,' she said.

'Necklace?'

The little girl laughed excitedly.

'The little blue necklace you promised me, Meja,' she told him. 'Where is it?'

Meja's heart faltered. His head started aching and for a moment he thought he was going to black out. He made a bubbling sound with his mouth and held the little girl tighter.

'You promised you would buy me a little blue necklace when you got a job,' the girl told him.

Of course Meja remembered. That was years back when he left school and went to the city to look for a job. His little sister had cried for she loved him and in a spurt of tenderness he had promised her a beautiful blue necklace for her little neck. But then he had promised lots of others things to other people too. If they all remembered too . . . Now his mind exploded into bitterness. Bitterness against himself and everybody. Where is the necklace? It kept repeating over and over again. The necklace.

He shook his head to clear it.

'Did you bring it?' the tiny voice insisted.

Meja shook his head negatively.

'But . . .' the girl complained.

'Yes, I know that I promised,' he said almost to himself.

The girl looked up into his face, her face twisted in anxiety. Tears welled behind her eyes. Meja noticed this and he felt himself suddenly overwhelmed with disappointments, his own and hers . . .

'Who is at home?' he asked her.

'Mama is there,' she cried. 'And the others too.'

Meja swallowed.

'Father?' he asked.

'He is not in,' she told him.

'Where is he?'

The girl fought to suppress the tiny sobs that shook her little body.

'He went to my uncle's,' she told him, 'to borrow money for my school fees.' Then her fingers dug into his neck with excitement, the tears forgotten. 'I go to school, Meja,' she said.

School, money, fees, school, necklace, swam through his head. Only they made too much sense the way they were, confused. That was what hurt. Yes, they made sense that hurt.

'I started last year,' the girl went on. 'I know how to write, read and count.'

'Really?' Meja tried to concentrate.

'Yes,' she told him. 'And father says that if I read well I can also come to the city and get a job like you.'

Meja's head gave a thud and the tremors returned.

'Do you want to see me write, Meja?' his little sister asked him.

Meja nodded.

She released herself from his arms and walked to the path and sat down. Meja remained where he was. She called him to go and see but he did not hear her. She ran back to where he was leaning on the post and pulled him by the hand.

'Come see,' she cried.

He let himself be led limping to the path. Her quick eyes did not fail to notice the limp, though he tried to conceal it.

'You are hurt?' she asked raising her wide-eyed face to his.

'No,' he said quickly.

Then he saw where her thin finger had traced on the dust on the path: W A B U I

The writing was twisted and childish as though a tiny little worm had accidentally formed the word on the dust. Meja watched it and his head ached. He knelt by the path.

'See,' she said. 'I can write my name.'

'Is that your name on the dust?' he asked.

She put her hands behind her back, regarded him seriously and nodded.

Meja shook his head.

'It is not spelt that way,' he said. 'Here, let me show you.'

He stretched out one scarred hand and wrote next to her writing: W A M B U I.

'See?' he asked, his hand still on the dust.

She did not answer. She stood staring at his malformed hand. He looked down and saw what she was staring at.

'Your hand,' she was saying.

But he did not hear her. His head was swimming again. Memories flew through his head; school, books, offices, dustbins, dustbins, dust . . . There his mind faltered. He dug his fingers into the dust to support himself. Then he withdrew his scarred hand and dug it into his pocket to hide it.

But the girl was still staring.

'Write, write, count,' he told the little girl from far off.

The girl at once forgot all about the hand and started inscribing on the dust: 1 2 3 4 . . .

She raised her eyes to her kneeling brother.

'Shall I write your name?' she begged.

He nodded. He looked in the direction of home. Through the maize and banana plants that hemmed it in, he could just make out his father's house. So near, yet so far away. Smoke rose from the hut and lazily coiled its way into the unfriendly late afternoon air. Yet inside the hut, he felt, warmth and love and familiness flourished. So near, yet so far away.

He thought about his mother at home cooking for the children and his father gone to beg for school fees. And here he was, scarred and afraid of going home. He dared not face them. The little sister remembered about the necklace. How much more would the others remember? Would they understand how he failed to get the job? And the scars and the limp and tattered clothes and battered body and, no! He just could not explain.

As he stared at the fine brown dust and the tiny finger that snaked its path of knowledge on it, tears flooded his eyes. His body shuddered.

He remembered how high-spirited the family had all been when he had first left school to go and work in the city. Their son and brother was going to work and earn money and . . . and buy blue little necklaces.

Years of hopelessness passed through his mind and he saw in them two youths loitering around the dustbins in the backstreets. Almost a year and a half of eating rubbish; then months on a hospital bed. Then he remembered the journey home from the hospital and the nice nurse who had given him the fare home. She had been good and had understood without any need for a lot of explanation. There were some good souls still around although they were scarce, especially in the city. Of the borrowed money now only one shilling remained in his pocket and that was hardly enough for a necklace of any colour. Neither could it help pay for the school fees.

The little sister, one arm on her big learned brother's shoulder, struggled with her knowledge and drew comfort from his presence.

'M ... M .. M,' she said and a scrawny hand scratched a bony head. 'Show me how to write your name, Meja,' she told him.

Automatically the scarred right hand shot out of the pocket and started writing on the dust. The little girl was again hypnotised by the hand with its shiny scars and twisted nails.

'Your hand,' she said again. 'Let me see.'

Before he could hide it she lifted the torn hand in hers and scrutinised it, fright paralysing her face. She looked at the crooked hand and the bones that showed through the skin.

'What happened to it?'

'Nothing,' he moaned.

His heart started racing again. His mind whirled. Dustbins flew through it, cars, policemen, cars, people and ... at the back of his mind brakes screamed.

The little girl released his hand and bent down to see what he had written. Something dropped on the dust among the writing. One, two, three drops and she looked up again.

Meja's body was quite rigid and tears flowed down his cheeks. His muscles were tense and at the corners of his mouth a little froth formed.

At the back of his mind he seemed to hear a car honk. He spun round instinctively and accidentally threw the little girl to the ground. But down the cold evening path nothing moved. With a cry of despair the boy collapsed on the grass.

The girl looked at the motionless body, very frightened. She picked herself up and tried to turn her brother over on to his back.

'Meja ... Meja,' she cried.

But he did not move. She lifted his head and looked into the hurt face. Then with one last look at his scarred hand still gripping a handful of grass with which he had tried to support himself, she turned and ran towards home.

'Mother ... Mother,' she cried. 'He is dead, mother. He is dead.'

A few moments later she returned with an old, worn, unbelieving and excited mother and a few other people. They came running from the forest of maize and banana plants and they were breathless when they came to the fork on the path. The sun was going down fast and a shadow fell on the ground so that they could just about see where the little Wambui was pointing. About three feet from the fork on the dirty dust were some inscriptions:

W A B U I

W A M B U I.

1 2 3 4

M E J A.

And close to the writing on the dust an old battered shilling stared back at them.

That was all. There was neither Meja nor anyone else. Meja had fled. And he had left behind neither a beautiful blue necklace nor money for school fees. But he had left them all his wealth. All the money he had brought back from the city after years of absence. One dirty old shilling that was still a shilling.

9

DARKNESS CAME FAST in the country and as though it were a sign the crickets took up their chorus of undirected song. Here and there a hyrax sent out a contented groan followed by an ear-shattering scream that for a moment silenced the whole night. It was a cloudless sky and the whole universe was uncurtained for the world to see. A light wind was blowing with all the chill that only a country wind could carry and the birds in their nests by the roadside twittered their protest.

Meja's feet were cold on the soft dust of the road and his knee was beginning to ache. He held his tattered clothes protectively around himself in an effort to keep out the chill but the wind managed to get through the thin clothing. His teeth chattered uncontrollably and for a time he let them be. Then he clenched them tight and with his jaws aching a little he limped along the lonely road.

His mind was full of bitterness. His home and family were now a mere scar in his past. Their problems and necklaces and school fees meant little to him now. That he had been so close to his home and then turned round without seeing his parents was no longer a matter for feeling. There was no room for such feeling in his mind. All there was was the determination to get away from the past and back to the city. What to do once he got back there he did not know. The point was to get away from the country and meetings with twelve-year-old girls that were no bigger than two-year-olds. Away from the red earth and the maize plantations and all. Maybe once back in the city he would try to trace his companion Maina again and the two would go back to the backstreets and enjoy life again just as before.

It was twelve-odd miles to the main road that crossed the country road at right angles and ran due south to the city, and on due south-east to the unknown. It was for this main road that Meja was aiming. Once on it there was a chance that he might get a lift on a passing vehicle. So for most of the night he struggled with himself and headed towards the highway and away from his home. It was about three o'clock when cold and hungry and worn he came to the highway, and sat down on the dewy wet grass to rest by the side of the road. Until the morning traffic got under way there would be no lift for him and he thought of making himself comfortable for the wait. Just then the moon rose from the tops of the high hills to the east, high and bright.

Its light seemed to carry an unnatural chill of its own and the night by the highway felt cold and terrifying. Meja now shivered so much that he could not sit still. His tired muscles started aching and he feared they might cramp.

He stood up, stretched himself and looked around. A few yards from the road on either side, the bush lay and watched him as though with a million terrifying eyes. The road itself stretched like a cold black serpent to the left and right as far as the first bends a few miles on either side of him. And as far as he could see there was no traffic on it. He sat down on the grass again but the wind had now increased and he had to find shelter. A drain ditch ran alongside the road, grass-covered and dry as it always was during the dry season. He settled into the ditch and there, where the wind rarely reached, it was warmer. To get his head completely out of the wind he lay on his back staring at the cold black expanse of the mysterious heavens.

As he watched, a shooting star detached itself from a galaxy and went spitting fire across the sky to another galaxy further to the south-west. The crickets kept up their song and a little way down the road where the road traversed a perennial swamp, frogs croaked in a sort of inter-swamp croaking competition. These kept the tired traveller's mind ringing with their irregular knocking sound. And then to increase the misery, attracted by the smell of warm human blood, the mosquitos from the swamp invaded him. They came in squadrons and landed on every exposed patch of skin on his body. Meja covered his face with his hand and they stung his hands until they itched maddeningly. He twisted his body and turned but fresh reinforcements arrived with more poisonous stings. When he was exhausted, he turned on to his belly, buried his face and hands in the long grass and fell into a troubled sleep.

He was awakened at about dawn after only a few hours' sleep. The early country-city traffic was in full swing and it was the rumbling of the heavy trucks carrying goods for the city markets that awakened him. The ground under him trembled violently as the laden vehicles tried to get a powerful grip on the rough tarmac. Occasionally a car passed along as people who had business tried to get to the city before the offices opened.

Meja pulled himself out of the ditch. His crippled right leg was cramped painfully and he bit his lower lip trying to stretch it out. Pain seared his leg and a sharp twang registered itself on his hip. Then his mangled hand cramped too and he clenched his teeth painfully trying not to scream. Slowly both cramps dissolved into warm tremors and he was able to stand up.

Way off to the east where the moon had risen the night before, the sky was reddening. Birds were waking up along the bush lining the road. It would be a full hour before the sun rose.

From round the first bend a large vehicle changed gears noisily and came snorting down the road. Meja took a deep breath and stepped right into the glare of its headlights. He started waving his hands, but the truck came right on showing no signs of stopping. Meja had to jump off the road to save himself.

Meja's heart sank to the bottom of his stomach. Sweat stood on his face at the effort he had put into avoiding being run over by the truck. He shook his head at the realisation of his hopelessness and rubbed the sweat off his face. Getting a lift was not going to be as easy as he had thought. He started limping towards the city, but after struggling for two miles he could walk no further and he sat on the grass again to rest. The early morning wind came and went and he was rested. He jumped back on to the road and tried for a lift again. The third vehicle he tried was a quarry lorry and this one stopped for him. He limped round to the cab and spoke to the driver.

'Going to the city?' he asked.

The driver regarded him for a full second, from the ragged clothes and the ragged body to the tired looking face. Then he shrugged away his curiosity and spoke without taking the cigarette from the corner of his mouth.

'Hop on it if you are going and stop asking stupid questions,' he said.

The cab was already occupied by two men and the driver, and Meja limped to the back of the truck. He struggled with his weak body before a turn boy emerged from the mass of tarpaulin on board and helped him by pulling him by the wounded hand. Hardly had he pulled his leg from the huge wheel than it started turning and they were off. The lorry lurched and sent Meja and the turn boy to the floor.

'Over here,' the turn boy told Meja and dived into a large canvas sheet right under the back view window of the cab. Here the wind was less and it was almost warm.

They lay there in the dust choking and sneezing as the lorry gathered speed and shot towards the city. They could not have talked even had they wanted to. The truck made a thundering rattle and roll and they were thrown here and there under the tarpaulin as they swept round corners at breakneck speed.

It seemed only a short time later when the truck jolted to a stop. Thinking that it might have stopped only momentarily the two men lingered under the tarpaulin. The doors of the cab opened and banged back and they heard the occupants moving about on the gravel outside. The turn boy peeped from under the warm dusty covering first. Then he wriggled out of it.

'We have arrived,' he said to Meja.

Meja wondered as he found his way from under the coverings. He had heard neither the city traffic nor its general noise. How then could they have arrived and so soon? Or had they made a wrong turning some place along the road? He eventually found his way from under the coverings and rose to his feet on the truck.

He held his breath and then let it hiss out through his nostrils. All round the truck were mounds of gravel of all types and sizes. A few yards away was a rocky cliff which rose close to two hundred feet and stretched for yards in each direction. On one side of the truck was the crusher built into the rocky cliff. It was a collection of wood and iron sheeting and a few stones and there was movement all round it.

Meja stood for a time and watched the rock factory. Then he looked at the turn boy on the ground watching him with interest. He jumped off the high body of the truck and stood next to him.

'We are three miles from the city,' the man told him. 'I will show you a short cut. Come.'

It was about six in the morning. The air was still moisty cold and the sun was just rising. The quarry man led him round the mounds of gravel and along a path that led out of the quarry. The path traversed the smaller side of the cliff and along its wall to a slight plain above. Meja was panting with exertion when they came to the top. And from where they stood the city was clearly visible lying in the morning mist. A dark smoky haze hung over it and the many-coloured lights looked weak and faint. Most of them were just beginning to go out, as though snuffed out by the early morning chill.

'The driver does not go into the city early in the mornings or he could have taken you down there,' the stone-digger told Meja. 'He has to wait for the first load of gravel to the city. But it is not very far as you can see. You will be there before the sun gets hot. Just follow this path until you come again to the main road. A few yards along the road on your left, the path is continued. After crossing the small river you will be right in the city. You can't lose the way.'

Meja stood undecided for a long time. The quarry man watched him quietly. Meja shook his head to try and concentrate.

'Are you all right?' the other asked him.

Meja nodded.

'Is there anything I can do for you?'

Meja looked at him, looked away to the city, and back at him. He started to say something, then stopped. Only now that he was in the city, he did not know what to do or where to go and he was a little frightened. He was attacked by the same kind of terror that had assailed him the first time he came, the same kind of fear, fear of the tall buildings, the mainstreets and the people that dwelt in them.

'Thank you for the lift,' he said to the man.

Summoning his last bit of courage he started walking away. After limping a few paces he stopped. He thought for a few seconds and then limped on. The other man watched him go.

'Goodbye,' he said. There was nothing else to say.

'Bye-bye,' Meja said without turning.

But at the other's words his movements became slower. His mind was thinking but very slowly. The good-heartedness of the other man was obvious. Maybe the man could have helped him. It would be foolish to go away still in need if the quarry man could assist him out of his problems. Maybe he was losing a good future friend. He stopped and turned round.

But the quarry man was not there. He had gone back to his work quite unaware of the other's need for him. For a moment, Meja was panic-stricken. His need and the possibility of losing the chance of help terrified him. But the man had gone, and Meja was quite alone.

He started running back to the quarry. He limped down the precarious cliff path and had his feet and hands cut by the sharp rock. His hands and feet aching and bleeding, he caught up with the man, who on hearing pebbles rolling behind him turned round. A song he was whistling froze on his lips. Then he recognised the ragged figure that was Meja and his face broke into an enquiring grin.

'You scared me,' he said.

Meja stopped confused, his hands on the rock-face supporting himself and his legs trembling slightly. He felt like turning round and running but his legs did not move. The two stared at one another for a spell.

'Can I help you, friend?' the other asked, the grin disappearing.

Meja swallowed and the feeling of hopelessness weighed down on him more heavily.

'You want me to direct you to some place?' the quarry man asked.

Meja shook his head.

'I am in difficulties,' he mumbled.

The other looked him up and down and wondered what crime the pitiable creature might have committed.

'Trouble with police?' he asked.

Meja shook his head.

'Well?'

'Job.'

The other man did not understand.

'I . . . I . . .' Meja told him. 'Can you get me a job? Here in your place?'

The other screwed his face deep in thought. He studied Meja again.

Then he shook his head. Then he noticed Meja's plight and desperation and he spoke up quickly.

'I don't know,' he said, 'but we could check. We need a few more people to replace another lot that was killed in an accident. We could see the foreman about it but . . .' He looked Meja up and down. 'It is not easy work this. Why don't you try getting a job some other place?'

Meja was at once conscious of his weak condition. And he was very hungry too.

'I have tried to get a job before,' he said.

He shook his head negatively.

The other sighed. He was very quick in understanding.

'Let us go see the foreman,' he said.

Meja followed the new-found friend down the rocky precipice to the gravel mounds again. The lorry in which they had come was still in the same position they had left it. At the office next to the crusher the other miners were queued to have their cards stamped so that they could start work. Meja had not thought the quarry employed so many people. He noticed that they had one thing in common: besides being ragged and dust caked, all the miners were large and muscular and very much unlike himself. Some of the huge stone-miners were already walking along the sheer cliff to their work areas, their heavy steel mallets and picks slung over their shoulders.

Meja and his friend fell behind the queue quietly. The boisterous fellows in front of them talked and laughed loudly as they tossed their cards through the pigeon-hole to be checked and stamped ready for collecting when the day's work was over. Few of them even seemed to notice Meja, a midget among them. The whole area was now full of noise and movement. Someone started the crusher and a confusion of thunderous noise and white dusty powder filled the air. Only Meja and his companion were at the pigeon-hole now.

'Hello, Ngigi,' the man behind the pigeon-hole saluted in a booming voice.

'Hello, boss,' Meja's friend answered handing in his blue work card.

It was stamped and filed but Ngigi still lingered.

'How is the mother of Njeru?' the foreman asked of his wife.

'She is fine,' Ngigi told him.

'And the little boys?'

'Them too,' Ngigi told him.

Then he hesitated.

'Boss,' he said. 'I have a friend here. Can you fix him up with a job?'

'Sure, sure,' the foreman said. 'That is quite right. Is he as huge as you are?' he enquired. 'Let me come out there.'

103

At the mention of Ngigi's size, Meja noticed it for the first time. Though slightly shorter than him, Ngigi was thicker and more solidly built than Meja. Under the dusty clothes he wore Ngigi had a body that was many times stronger than that of Meja.

A door set in the opposite wall of the small office opened and the grotesque foreman came through it. He was dressed in a brown sports shirt that bulged under the pressure of his muscles. He stood almost a foot taller than Meja and his neck and arm muscles were extremely large. His legs and thighs stuck out of his shorts like huge tree trunks. Veins covered every visible part of his skin and danced as his great quantity of blood coursed through their many valves. Meja thought he had never seen so much muscle accumulated in one single person.

The giant foreman stopped in mid-step and regarded Meja from head to foot. He glanced at Ngigi a sneer on his face, but the other refused to meet his eyes.

'Is this a joke or something?' he asked.

'He wants a job,' Ngigi said. 'Ask him.'

The foreman looked down at Meja. He took in thread arms, legs with bones almost showing through the skin. He shook his head.

'I want a job,' Meja said.

The foreman looked from Meja to Ngigi and noticed that the two were serious.

'But we can't give you a job here,' he said. 'How heavy are you? Oh it is useless. You can't weigh more than a hundred pounds. What could you possibly do here with that sort of muscle? We just can't have you.'

'But I can work. Hard,' Meja pleaded.

The foreman shook his head.

'It is no use arguing,' he said. 'We don't have any work for people like you. Look at Ngigi here. What we need is sheer brute strength, nothing more. I know you want to work. So does everybody else. But it takes more than will to wield that hammer you see there. To lift the pick alone needs more than will. We have no job for you. I am sorry, Ngigi.'

Ngigi said nothing to help him out. He could see for himself that Meja's chances for the job were very slim. He couldn't even push a wheelbarrow full of rock from the look of him. Not with that kind of muscle.

But Meja was determined.

'I promise I will . . .' he began to say.

'No use friend, no use,' the foreman said, trying to sound gentle. 'Look at that rocky face over there,' he told him.

They all looked at the high cliff with its many jagged faces. It stood tall and solid and stared defiantly back at them. Meja could almost see it breathing power, unbeatable and unbreakable. Almost like the barrel shoulders of the foreman and his miners.

'See what I mean?' the foreman said. 'It is almost invincible, that rock is. I hate to look at it myself. It seems endlessly strong. And that is what you are asking to go against, armed with a pick I am not sure yet you can lift.' He shook his big head. 'No I will not give you the job. I cannot.'

Meja struggled with his thoughts and almost cried. He had reached the point of turning round and going away defeated when Ngigi jumped in to help him.

'You can give him probation, boss,' he said.

The foreman whirled round to him.

'What?' he cried then turned to Meja. 'It is useless I tell you. I appreciate your spirit, but it is useless trying. You can't pass the interview. You will waste your time and unless you pass the test there is no pay for the work done. You go . . .'

'Let him try, boss,' Ngigi said without looking up.

'Please . . .' Meja said.

'I say . . .' the foreman shook his head. 'Oh, hell. What have I got to lose? All right. Take that pick and mallet. Ngigi, get him a bag of wedges.'

Ngigi went in search of wedges, satisfied that they had given the poor man a chance. If he believed he could work in the quarry maybe he could. Meja stood by the foreman and stared at the mocking rock-face. It still grinned stupidly back at him.

'See that wall,' the foreman told him. 'When the wedges are brought you will have to hew out of that cliff nine cubic feet of rock at least. That is the test.' Then he changed his tone. 'Why don't you go try creating some more muscle then come back?'

Meja did not answer. He swallowed hard and wondered where big muscle was created on empty stomach. He did not ask this though. The foreman would not understand. Nobody in the world would understand his problems. No one except, yes, Maina could. Only he had fallen into the darker side of life with him. All the others just saw days come and go as usual, and the moon rise and set as always. But to Meja every dawning day meant more pain and more hopeless wondering in the world of the lost.

Ngigi brought the bag of heavy steel wedges.

'Go measure out for him,' the foreman told him. 'I will come to see when it is done.'

Then, his large muscles contracting and expanding like a mass of steel cables, he walked away shaking his huge head.

The two watched him go. Ngigi too shook his head.

'He told you what you will have to do?' he asked.

Meja nodded and swallowed.

Ngigi led the way carrying the bag of wedges. Meja struggled with the mallet and pick and his lame hand. The crusher roared with laughter at his futile efforts to lift both tools on to his shoulders and its choking breath was the white powder of the rock it munched so hungrily. And the solid rock cliff on the opposite side twisted its many jagged faces in contempt. Sweat poured down his face as with one tool on his shoulder and the other dragged along the ground, he panted into the dust after Ngigi.

Men, real men, with bulging sinews and lots of willpower and life moved around him carrying their picks and mallets as though they were made of light wood. And none of them gave any thought to the puny half-man who struggled in the choking dust towards his interview point, dragging his tools along the ground.

He caught up with Ngigi round the gravel hillocks. Ngigi stopped to watch him. Critically he shook his head and lifted the pick to his own shoulder as though it was made of rubber instead of solid steel. Then he led the way along the cliff wall and Meja followed. All along the wall men were at work with their picks and mallets, and the sound of steel ringing upon steel filled the air. Most of the men sang loudly as they worked. As the sound of the crusher fell behind them, the sound of song and mallets and swearing replaced it. The men had already managed to dig caverns for themselves on the rock mass and were now fighting to expand these before the day became hotter and stamina decreased. Some of the men stopped to watch the two go by and a few whistled in surprise.

A quarter of a mile up away from the crusher, the pit became narrower and they came to the end of the rocky ravine. There was no one working at this end and it was quiet, almost lonely. The walls of the deep rock gully came so close together they gave Meja the feeling of being locked up in a tiny cell with sharp protuberances on the wall and the sky for a ceiling. The noise of the stone-eating machine carried faintly to this end of the pit and the songs of men working along the line were even fainter.

Ngigi threw the pick to the ground with a metallic ring. Meja threw the mallet down too and stood panting.

'Well,' he said. 'Here we are. I brought you to this area so that you can work alone in peace. You could never possibly get anywhere out there with the other boys. They would laugh you into stupidity. Here you are all alone by yourself. Start working now if you want to get anywhere before the sun goes higher and becomes hotter.'

Meja stood worried. He was already exhausted from the journey along the ravine.

'How do I . . .' He did not know what he wanted to ask. There were

106

so many things he did not know and many more he did not understand.

Ngigi pointed at the rock face next to him.

'You can start anywhere on that face,' he said. 'There is no formula to digging nine cubic feet of rock out of this hell. How you do it is of no importance. Just do it.'

Meja looked at the infinite expanse of rock.

'But you are supposed to measure it out for me,' he said.

Ngigi shook his head.

'It is useless before you have started getting anywhere,' he told him. 'You have got everything you need. Pick, wedges, mallet and will. Just lift that mallet and bash it against the rock. I will come back and see how you are getting on.'

He turned after nodding to Meja and started walking away.

Meja threw one last quick shy glance at the cliff and lifted the mallet with all his energy so that he had no strength left to smash it against the rock. He let it fall weakly on the wall and it bounced off and passed to within a few inches of his lame leg. He lifted it a second time and with the same result.

Ngigi had stopped to watch concealed by a corner of the wall. He came back running.

'Are you all right?' he asked.

Meja nodded full of embarrassment.

'That is no way to deal with rocks,' Ngigi told him. 'Here let me show you. You must be careful not to hurt yourself.'

His hands pulsated with strength and he spat on them to get a firmer grip on the mallet handle. He pushed his right hand right next to the head of the mallet while the left hand held the handle way back.

'You hold it this way,' he said. 'Then . . .'

He whipped the mallet back and brought it down on the rock. Fragments of rock flew into the air in all directions. He hit the rock twice and a small heap of rocks lay at his feet.

'The rock is tough and obstinate,' he said, dropping the mallet. 'You have got to meet strength with strength. Hit it hard. You cannot afford to be kind to this kind of primitive strength. Keep trying.'

Meja picked up the mallet again.

'No, do not hold it that way,' Ngigi said. 'Bring your hands. . . .'

Then he noticed the poor condition of Meja's wounded hand and stopped. On his face was written the same kind of curious horror Meja had seen on the face of his little sister.

'What happened to it?' he asked.

'An accident,' Meja said, his body cold and numb.

He had tried his best to conceal the wounded hand from everybody including the foreman, and now that Ngigi had seen it he wondered whether they would let him go on working. Ngigi stood looking at the disfigured hand almost afraid to touch it.

'What kind of an accident?' he asked.

'It's nothing,' Meja told him.

In his subconscious mind he heard the honk of that fatal car and instinctively spun round. The brutal rock looked down on him and smiled solidly but there was no vehicle anywhere. Sweat stood on his face and his hands trembled. He turned round and faced Ngigi again, his fear and anger and confusion burning in his eyes as though they were directed at him.

'Are you all right?' Ngigi enquired again, eyeing him suspiciously.

Meja swallowed his confusion and took the mallet away from him.

'Yes,' he said. 'I am all right.'

'Well, you know what to do,' Ngigi told him and backed away. 'I must go to my work now. As I said, there is no set formula. Just barrel into that rock.'

This time he did not even look back. He walked away shaking his head and wondering. If only he could understand what drove the poor man to such desperation. He very much wondered.

Meja stood and let the shivers run out of his body. He stared at the rock as one would stare at an enemy he knew was his superior, yet did not want to admit the fact to himself. Slowly his desperation turned to anger and then to hate. Great hate which whistled with his breath out of his nostrils. And it was all directed at the rock wall that would not give way.

'I am all right,' he whispered to himself. 'I am all right.' Then he screamed. 'I am all right.'

As his cry of self-inspiration rang faintly through the gully, it was picked up and magnified a thousand times by the rocky cliff so that it too seemed to shout back to him that it was all right. Only its voice was louder because its strength was recognised by the miners and it had a lot of self confidence. This made Meja angrier. His hate rose to a peak and like a frenzied devil, he started lifting the huge mallet and throwing himself against his enemy that held back its little pebbles that spelt money, which in turn meant freedom from hunger and hopelessness.

Like a maniac he swung the mallet back and forth until his hands were raw and blistered and his body ached from toe to head. Sweat sprang from all over his body and his clothes stuck to him. His mouth was sticky and the pain in his middle had grown into a dull feeling. Even the distant roar of the crusher could not penetrate his concentrated senses.

The sun rose higher and became very hot. It sank into Meja's body and even the rocks creaked as heat seeped into them. He worked on regardless. And when he was weak and spent so that he could hardly breath, he staggered back and regarded the work he had done. It was approximately equal to nothing. The rock stood in front of him very much intact, except for the dent his friend had made. At this realisation, he sat down in a defeated haze, leaned on the rock itself and closed his eyes.

He was awakened by Ngigi a few hours later. It was lunchtime and Meja could share Ngigi's lunch with him. Together they walked slowly back to the crusher leaving the tools at the diggings. All the miners converged on the crusher joking and laughing loudly as usual. The crushing machine was switched off, the dust settled and the food packets were opened. And now there was very little talk among the tired stone diggers as they explored their food parcels. Meja ate hungrily and Ngigi, seeing the starved look about him, reduced his own speed of eating to give him time to get ahead.

When food was eaten the miners lay around in the shade of the crusher and tried for siestas. Most of them were half naked having left their shirts in the working areas. Cigarettes were lit. Meja watched the strong bodies from the corner of his eye and wondered how they had managed to grow that big.

'Do you smoke?' Ngigi asked him offering him a cigarette.

Meja shook his head.

'Do you think I will make it?' he asked.

Ngigi lay back and stretched his body in the shade. He pulled at his cigarette and let the smoke come slowly out of his nostrils and half-closed lips.

'It is hard to say right now,' he said. 'There is still a lot of day left. We stop work at six.'

There was silence.

Meja looked round at the miners lying carelessly in the shade. Some of them were already asleep. The only place he had seen so satisfied an atmosphere was at the farm he had worked on with Maina. And there too they had had a foreman, and he was very hard to please.

'Don't you think you should have measured out my part for me?' he enquired feeling the raw palms which like the rest of his body were caked in dust.

Ngigi shook his head.

'No use,' he told him. 'When you have dug out nine cubic feet of rock you will certainly know,' he laughed lightly. 'You will not be able to lift an eyelid.'

Meja sighed and stood up.

'I think I had better go continue,' he said.

Ngigi turned and looked at him idly with only one eye open.

'Listen my friend, eh,' he began to say.

'Meja Mwangi,' the other told him.

'Yes, Meja,' Ngigi went on. 'Just take it easy. It is rocks you are fighting against not people. You have got to make use of tact as well as strength. You cannot hurt the rock by any feelings. It understands nothing less than strength. Just go about it cleverly. Follow the line of weakness on the rock and you will bring the whole mountain down. Otherwise you will kill yourself.'

Meja stood and looked at his friend. He saw his sister tiny and weak and asking for a necklace. How could Ngigi ever understand this and all the rest? How could anybody ever?

He turned round and hobbled back to his working station thinking hard. Somehow he had to burrow three feet into the cliff. How he was going to do it he did not know. And neither did anyone else for that matter. It was obvious no one had any confidence in his strength. He was in it alone equipped only with a lot of will. He looked down at the morning's diggings. His body ached at the thought of what he had yet to do. Like in a dream, he picked his oversized mallet and swung it to his shoulders. He stared at a particular spot on the rough and ugly rock and concentrated on centering all his force on it. His arms and hands and back ached and this distracted his aim. The hammer bounced off the rock and thudded on the small bag holding the wedges. He picked up the small bag of wedges, took one strong wedge out of it and weighed it in his scarred hand.

In his mind he heard Ngigi's words: 'Follow the line of weakness and you will bring the whole mountain down.'

Then the meaning of the words dawned on his mind. Going down on one knee he started studying the rock face. He scratched it with the edge of the steel wedge and blew away the dust and scratched again. Sweat got into his eyes and stung them. Rubbing it away with the back of his hand he went on searching, searching, searching. And at long last when hope was beginning to wane and depression to settle in again, he found them.

They were two faint cracks that crossed at right angles on the rock-face and grew fainter as they lengthened in different directions. They were so faint he had to mark them before looking away or he would have lost them. But they were cracks all right and a weakness.

Meja took two more heavy wedges from the bag and using the blunt side of one as a hammer he knocked the other into one of the cracks. The other wedge he wedged into the other crack. Then he stepped back and studied his work. It was not very bad. He lifted the heavy mallet. He concentrated his thoughts just as before and this time the hammer did not bounce off. The wedge slipped in some inches. The other wedge also needed only one bang and it too slipped a few inches into the rock. The cracks grew deeper and wider. He rubbed his hands

110

in suspense. 'Follow the line of weakness . . .' his mind kept ringing.

Way back into the ravine the crusher restarted and its roar flowed in waves to the furthest corner of the pit and then rebounded. This was the sign to go back to work after lunch but Meja was already at work and needed no awakening. Even gigantic boulders had weaknesses where they lacked in feelings.

He collected the pick which up to now had been useless. Aiming at the enlarged crack he buried its tip three inches into the rock. He twisted and the crack lengthened to about seven feet from the ground. The horizontal one also expanded.

Meja's hands started bleeding and the dust got into them and the pain was almost unendurable. He clenched his teeth, dug his bare feet into the sharp splinters on the ground and twisted the handle of the pick.

The pick came away to his left and his own force turned him round and sent him backwards on to the opposite wall of the gully. There was a roar like of thunder and almost a ton of rock and dust came cascading down. Meja saw it come and flew out of the narrow end. The falling rockface filled most of the narrow end of the gully. His tools, pick, mallet and all were buried under the enormous mass of rock. For a moment he was frightened. He did not understand what had happened and he did not know how much of the rockface it was right to bring down. And for a long moment he stood leaning on the rock swaying and letting the pain run itself into nonexistence. He even closed his eyes and tried to doze.

Somebody exclaimed behind him and he was instantly wide awake. He turned to stare into a half circle of miners headed by the foreman. They had all heard the cascade which went ringing from wall to wall and had come to investigate. And Ngigi was among them.

'Well, well,' boomed the gigantic foreman, 'however did you do that?'

Meja was now nervous and confused at the same time.

'I did not . . .' he started to say.

'I can hardly believe you did it myself,' the foreman said, patting him on the shoulder. 'I could have sworn . . . You have just passed the probation and now I have no choice but let you have the job.'

Meja stood still and let everybody express his doubts and those who had any to spare, admiration. Then each with a last glance at the bony wretch that had brought down a mountain, they went back to their stations and some ran for wheelbarrows on which to wheel the rock to the crusher.

'You have done enough work for today,' the foreman said looking down at Meja. 'I will issue you with a work card tomorrow morning.'

He gave Meja another look over, then ambled away in his ill-fitting clothes. Meja stood by Ngigi and thought. Here at last was a foreman who could be satisfied. He would have done very well at the farm, where work was lighter and the only place one needed the foreman's understanding was at the food queue.

'Are you all right?' Ngigi asked.

Meja's face broke into a worn grin. He nodded his head.

'I am all right,' he said. 'So much all right.'

Ngigi glanced at the collapsed rocks and then at Meja.

'Nothing is really impossible,' he shook his head. 'Tell me, my friend, how did you do it?'

Meja looked down at his blistered hands and the ache in them was sweet warm and pleasant. He smiled feeling genuinely happy.

'I . . . I,' he said, 'I followed the line of weakness.'

Ngigi laughed.

'I knew you would never believe it,' Meja told him. 'But that is exactly what I did.'

Meja was thinking happy thoughts as he followed Ngigi out of the end of the quarry. He had managed to get himself a job at last. The future did not seem all that bad. The only thing it now lacked was his home. He felt even without thinking about it that he could never go back there now. Not even if he got the best paid job in the world and had enough money to buy a million blue necklaces and satisfy everybody else in the family. Never. Far along the deep rocky ravine, the crusher groaned and droned as it tirelessly crushed rock. And its sound was no longer harsh and mocking as before to Meja's ears. It sounded as soft and purring as that of a friendly cat. Meja was proud that soon, very soon, that same monster would be happily crunching and munching and chewing and digesting the greatest sweetest amount of rock it had ever had – his own hard-earned rock.

10

THE GREEN VAN turned away from the main road and drove along the dust-road leading to the prison. It was late in the afternoon and the driver, feeling hot and tired, disregarded the thirty miles per hour speed limit. He sped along the drive and a cloud of dust hung undecidedly in the air behind the truck, until the cool mountain breeze came and pushed it down the hill and into the forest. At the heavily built gates half a mile further on, the van stopped, the gates were thrown open, and the driver turned into the inner compound. Over at the office he stopped, jumped out of the cab, stretched himself and yawned lazily.

The Chief Warder saw the prison van come and watched the usual driver step out. He watched the van and its driver for a moment wondering what they had brought him this time. He bet with himself which one of his usual boys had been brought back, then walked out of the office to find out. He walked deliberately slowly to the van driver.

'Another load of public headache?' he asked.

The driver shook his head rubbing sweat off his brow.

'Only one this time, I am sorry,' he answered.

'Why sorry?' the warder asked. 'Maybe you think I love dealing in these cases. Well, you are wrong. I don't. I hope it is not another flogging case.'

The driver shrugged.

'That is the only exercise you have time for, I suppose,' he said. 'You are lucky though. The judge saved you the toil.'

He walked round to the back of the van, pulling a large bunch of keys from his pocket. He selected one key, inserted it into the lock, turned and pulled the door back. He peered into the dark interior of the van.

'Out you come,' he commanded. 'We are home.'

The prisoner extricated himself from the back of the van and stood squinting in the glare of the sun. The Chief Warder stepped back and stood scrutinising him from head to foot, making sure not to miss anything.

The prisoner was a big man, just a little under six feet tall. His shoulders were sagging under a mountain of muscles. His neck was thick and held up a big head with a rough weathered face and a rough beard and hair. But it was not the physical features of the prisoner that attracted the warder's attention. It was his dress. He was crudely dressed in an old blanket.

The other prisoners who were going for their early supper stopped and watched the lone prisoner. Some of them joked about his attire and laughed loudly. It was obvious too that the prisoner was not used to wearing a blanket for he held it clumsily round his shoulders.

'Well, well,' the Chief Warder said through his breath. 'And what do we have here?'

The van driver did not answer him. He reached into his pocket and lit himself a cigarette.

'The name is in his entry forms,' he said. 'Or you can ask him if you want to know for sure.'

'I can't rely on that,' the warder said. 'These people can change names faster than the quickest chameleon can change colour.'

'Better give him his suit if it is ready,' the driver told him. 'He borrowed that blanket from the police and I am taking it back tomorrow morning.'

The Chief Warder spun round quickly.

'And what will he wear on his way out?' he asked surprised.

The driver shrugged, blowing a cloud of smoke.

'You can always produce an old sack from somewhere,' he advised. 'Or lend him one of your own blankets if you care that much how he goes back to his people.'

The warder led the blanketed prisoner, who walked with a noticeable limp, into the drab office and handed him a suit of starched white prison uniform. The prisoner was at first confused by the shorts which seemed to have neither back nor front and he stood naked up to the waist trying to make up his mind which end to make the front end. The warder noticed the confusion.

'Don't you people wear clothes where you come from?' he asked.

The prisoner spoke for the first time, without looking up.

'We wear clothes where we people come from,' he said. 'Not sacks like these.'

The warder regarded him with a critical eye.

'This is your first time in, is it not, son?' he asked.

'I am not your son,' the prisoner said gruffly.

'Your type always behaves like that the first time they are thrown into the bag,' the aged warder went on to say. 'You don't seem to understand where you are. You cannot afford to talk like that to the people who take care of you here.'

The prisoner tried to say something.

'Hold it,' the Chief Warder told him. 'I am telling you this for your own good. If you are wise you will listen and do as you are told.'

114

The driver walked into the office, a sheaf of papers in his hands. He looked at the changed prisoner and sniggered.

'Say, chief,' he said, 'did you know this particular bird was coming along? Those clothes were really meant for him.'

The warder did not speak to him. He took the prisoner's papers and got busy booking him.

NAME: MEJA MWANGI alias BARRACUDA.
AGE: 26
CHARGE: BREAKING AND ENTERING AND ROBBING.
SENTENCE: ONE YEAR AND SIX MONTHS.

The van driver folded the old police blanket under his arm and walked to his van. He drove out of the prison yard and back the way he had come to the highway that led back to the city.

The Chief Warder handed out the usual disciplinary speech to the new prisoner. And as usual the prisoner paid little attention to what he was being told. He stood there bored, shifting his feet in an annoying manner. Then the warder led him out of the office to give him a chance to learn his lesson the way they all seemed to like it – the hard way. He led him to the prisoners' compound and locked the barbed wire door behind him. When the door was closed behind him, the prisoner stood in his new uniform and surveyed what was going to be home for the next one and a half years. The other prisoners were coming back from their dinner and going to their cell blocks for the night, although it was only about a quarter past five o'clock. A few of them stopped and stared back at him just as hard as he stared at them. The warder stood on the other side of the locked gate watching the new prisoner.

'Be social,' he advised in a low tone so that only Meja heard him. 'Get among them and make friends. One year is a long time just to stand there and stare. Since you are here you might as well like the lot.'

Meja showed no sign of having heard the old man's advice. But though he did not want to admit it, it made a lot of sense. He had better like them or perish. But he still stood looking into the mass of lawbreakers trying to decide which one of them looked agreeable enough to make friends with. He would need help if he was going to trace his cell in the compound, where every building looked like the other, white-washed and formidable. He had his cell number. But where the hell was this cell number nine? He was hungry but no one had mentioned anything about his dinner. So he stood watching the prisoners and wondering.

'Meja,' someone called from among the prisoners and ran towards him.

Meja stepped back in shock and leaned on the barbed wire gate. He

115

stepped forward again and into Maina's arms. His mind flew back to the backstreets and dustbins and their stink of food. Maina was no less shocked. They shook hands and hugged and shook hands again, while prisoners and warders alike watched the two old friends curiously.

'Where have you been all this long?' Maina asked.

'Just around,' Meja answered him. 'Don't tell me you were expecting me or I will be disappointed.'

Maina laughed.

'I am very glad to see you, Meja,' he said, and wrung his hand a hundredth time.

'In here?' Meja asked and feigned surprise. 'You must be joking, man. I would rather have stayed out and missed you altogether than come to find you here.'

Maina also caught up with his old gay mood.

'Did you really have that much of a choice?' he enquired.

'Not really,' Meja answered and shrugged.

They both laughed then stopped abruptly in mid-laugh. They looked one another up and down.

'Is this really you, Meja?' Maina said. 'You have grown very big. Have they started throwing vitamin pills into the supermarket dish?'

Meja shook his head.

'I wouldn't know. I have not been there for ages,' he said.

'And where have you been?' Maina went on.

'You have asked that question already,' Meja told him.

'Seriously, Meja, what brought you here?' the other asked.

Meja shrugged.

'A prison van,' he said. 'And if my guess is right the same van brought you out here.'

'I am serious, Meja,' Maina said.

'Then show me where cell nine is and we can talk later,' Meja told him. 'There is a lot of time for talk. I am going to be here for a year and a half from today.'

Maina looked him up and down again. He read the number 9999 on his chest and shook his head.

'It is incredible,' he said.

'Why is it incredible?' Meja asked him. 'Did you have to bribe your way into this cage?'

'Come, I am also in cell nine,' Maina told him.

Maina led the way among the rows and rows of white-washed blocks of houses and eventually into the furthest block from the gate. But for tiny vents at the highest point in the walls there were no windows anywhere. Inside the block Maina led Meja along a row of cells to the furthest cell in the corridor. On the door of the cell was chalked in red capital letters, CELL 9999.

There were no beds in number nine and the floor was quite bare. Blankets and mats were folded into a neat pile in a corner. A dim light bulb hung high on the ceiling on a level with the air-vent. The green door of the cell was of steel and had no fastenings from the inside. The inside of the cell, like everything else in the prison, was white-washed.

'This is cell nine,' Maina said, sweeping his hand from left to right. 'The den of the most crooked ruffians in the country. In this cell they are supposed to be keeping the hardest of the hard cases. As you can see they lock it from the outside. This cell is for holding nine people and you are the ninth. Whatever it was you said to the old jailer I have no idea, but guessing from the fact that he dumped you in here, he did not like it. Too bad for you. Your mat and blanket are in here. They were left by our ninth member when they suddenly founded a murder charge on his head and went to hang him for it. Feel at home.'

Meja looked round the white-washed cell and could not get the feeling that he was in prison, let alone for one year. It was all so different from what he had imagined. More strange was the fact that he was in prison and in the same cell with his oldest friend. He felt funny, but one thing he was sure of, it did not feel like it was home. He walked over to the pile of blankets and sat down on it.

'You limp?' Maina asked him. 'Did they beat you up before they brought you here?'

Instinctively Meja heard that fatal honk and could not help looking behind. And there was only that white-washed wall crowding him in. Maina noticed his plight.

'What happened?' he enquired.

'Nothing,' Meja said, his head wondering far off in the past.

'Nothing?'

'Oh, stop bothering me,' Meja told him. 'I will tell you later.'

Maina nodded.

'I nearly forgot,' he said. 'One and half years is a hell of a long time. Take your time.'

Meja did not answer.

Then as though given a cue the other seven members of cell nine trooped in. They lined up across the floor just inside the door and stood quite still.

'You have come,' Maina said to them. 'We have a new cell-mate. An old friend of mine. His name is Meja.'

The men did not answer though they looked the newcomer up and down and across. In their smartly kept prison uniforms they looked like a troop of boy scouts on parade. The cell door was thrown back and locked from the outside. They did not look back. The peephole on the door was pushed open and a gruff voice counted them loudly.

Then the peephole was closed and the warder's footsteps receded down the corridor shouting orders and numbers. The seven lined up across the inside of the door in cell number nine did not move. They stood like soldiers, legs astride, hands behind backs and stared at Meja.

'Meja,' Maina said. 'Here are the boys.'

Meja nodded, scrutinising the boys. Maina started the introduction left to right in order. And with each person finished with, he either bowed low or saluted and fell out of the queue. The salute stirred something deep in Meja's memory. It reminded him of a farm he had worked in once, with its horses and cattle and pigs and orchards. It also reminded him of his fat boss and a mean foreman, a skeleton of a cook named Boi and a lean mischievous youth named Maina. The salute he received now was the same one Maina handed out to him when he had wanted to cover up anything mischievous. In spite of age, Maina had not changed much in character.

'On the extreme left is Chege,' Maina said.

'Two years in for the so-called rape,' Chege said. 'But I kept telling that monkey of a judge that she had agreed and . . .'

'Second in line is Ngugi,' Maina went on, cutting the other's argument short.

'Three years in for robbery with violence,' Ngugi said. 'I am glad to know Maina had a friend outside number nine.'

They were all introduced one after the other and each in turn seemed perfectly cheerful as he announced his crime and sentence. None of them was in for less than one year and none seemed to mind. They were happy where they were, the way they were. As one of them put it to Meja:

'Ninth time in for robbery without violence,' he announced. 'This time for two years and some patting across the bottom. And if that swine of a warder does not take it easy with the cane, I will not live long enough to make the tenth comeback.'

Most of the other prisoners laughed but Meja could not find anything funny in being thrown in time and again. The mats were unfolded, thrown down and the blankets distributed. Then they threw themselves on the mats in a row and covered themselves. Meja was lying between Maina and Chege, looking up at the dim bulb above. His mind was whirling. He was in prison and that was a fact. His friend Maina was in with seven others and that too was a fact. They all seemed happy and contented with life in prison. He wondered whether he might eventually come to like it too. If all one did in prison was eat and drink and get himself locked up and counted like cattle, things were not very bad. At least that was better than living in a quarry and burrowing in the rock for the rest of one's life.

He looked up at the roof and at the white-washed walls and then back to the high dim bulb. The others were silent, breathing lightly and waiting. He could almost feel the aura of suspense that hung around them. And he knew what they were waiting for. His story. His very untellable story. And he did not know wh^re to start so he waited for one of them to break the ice with a straightforward question. But the hard cases of number nine were harder than he thought. They did not speak. They just lay on their backs staring up at the ceiling and holding their breath. Waiting.

'Don't people undress before going to sleep here?' Meja asked.

'Undress?' Maina spoke to him. 'We do not sleep here. There is no time for that. We lie down and wait for the day when we shall all leave. When they close all prisons and send us all back home then maybe we shall try to sleep then.'

They all laughed nervously but Meja only smiled.

'Doesn't someone switch off the light then?' he asked.

'And let all the inmates of number nine escape in the ensuing darkness?' somebody asked.

Meja groaned.

'This is prison, my friend, and not a holiday camp,' Maina advised.

Meja's efforts to dodge the main subject were not being very effective.

'You do some sort of forced labour here?' Meja asked.

'Not in the least,' Ngugi answered from inside his blanket. 'Here we eat and sleep and get counted and locked in cells. Smooth life. Better than most hotels in town. There is no charge for it whatsoever.'

There was silence for a moment.

'Are you afraid of work, like myself?' Maina asked. 'I thought . . .'

'I am not afraid of work,' Meja interrupted. 'I am not afraid of any work at all. I have done more work than any of you has ever cared to even think of.'

'And what are you doing here then?' someone asked. 'This is no place for your type.'

'I am in for robbery, my friends,' Meja told them. 'But I did not just walk out and rob somebody the way most of you did. I first worked.'

He stopped and the others waited patiently.

'Tell us what you did,' Maina told him. 'From when we parted at the supermarket.'

Meja stopped to recollect his escapades. He was as eager now to tell his story as the others were to hear it.

'Well, it was like this,' he started. 'When you threw whatever it was at me . . .'

'Apples,' Maina interjected.

'Whatever it was I did not know,' Meja went on. 'Anyway the supermarket attendant . . .'

'You two worked in a supermarket?' Chege interrupted.

'Yes, we cleaned their rubbish bins,' Maina said.

'Should I stop and let somebody else tell the story instead?' Meja asked them.

If he was going to tell the story at all he was going to do it with some dignity. This was not one of their usual dirty little stories and it was going to be told and listened to with respect, at least to the person who had lived it, himself.

'Go on, tell us,' Maina coaxed him. 'No more interruptions.'

Meja sighed.

'There had better not be any more or someone else will have to finish off,' he said.

He paused for a moment to let what he had said settle. Then he started again.

'The attendant it seemed was interested in the apples,' he went on. 'He came after me when he saw me catch the parcel. I ran faster than I had thought I could. He was joined by more people in the chase and a policeman. They raced me all over the town. I was scared. They were hard to shake off and I did not know what to do next. So I kept running round and round in the backstreets in circles. Then suddenly I ran into a mainstreet and . . .'

Maina exclaimed and then apologised when Meja glanced at him. The others were now on their elbows looking in his direction attentively. They were excited by the insane look that now crowded Meja's face.

'It was so sudden I did not even believe it myself,' Meja went on. 'There were people everywhere and little room to run. And I was freezing with terror,' he sighed. 'I ran into the front end of a moving car,' he said and held up his scarred hand for everybody to see.

The inmates of number nine looked, saw the ugly hand and deflated slowly. They did not speak.

'I was lucky,' Meja went on. 'The car was not travelling very fast. Not many broken bones. Just snapped something in my right knee and my hand and acquired a multitude of scratches. I was in hospital for six long months while they fixed the fractures. The doctor said I will limp for the rest of my life.'

When he stopped the others looked at one another then back at him.

'The police?' Maina ventured.

'They came to the hospital all right,' Meja said. 'They wanted to know what I had taken. I told them I did not know. I had no time to look properly. They did not believe me. They gave up after a lot of questions. Then I healed. A nurse gave me some money for fare home when I told her my sad story.'

'Did . . .' Maina could not help himself.

He remembered Boi's farm and shivered.

Meja too remembered the pledge they had made at the farm and did not look at Maina when answering.

'Yes, I did go home all right,' he said. 'I had no other place to go and I couldn't find you at the back of the supermarket so I went home. But I only got as far as the gate to my home. There I met my sister and ... and ... then I felt that things would never be the same as before. I lost courage and turned back to the city. I did not see anyone else at home. Just that little girl.'

He paused. The others watched him and tried to read every thought that passed through his face even before he spoke it.

'I was scared of my own people,' Meja went on. 'I was given a lift back to the city although I had no idea what drew me there. I had to get as far away as possible from home. I made a friend and he got me a job in a quarry and,' at this point the grinding noise of the crusher passed through his mind and he squinted against the dust, 'we dug stones. At first I was weak and hungry but my friends cared for me until I could lift the tools and mine rocks like everybody else. It was a tiring job, but we got enough to eat and that was enough. We dug like monsters and the machine turned rock into gravel and food. I lived with my friend, Ngigi, in his little tin shack. He had a wife and little children, but he let me squeeze in. We ate together and mined together. There was a jolly crowd of rock-diggers out there.'

'On Saturday nights we held dances and drank liquor together. There were a few girls around the miners' camp and we danced with them and fought for them. They caused more trouble than the rocks did. You should have seen those mining giants fight with crowbars. They taught me how to fight too. I had to learn if I was going to keep alive and enjoy it. Policemen rarely came to the camp and when they did they only took away the visitors. So we worked, ate, drank and lived. Only we worked too hard. Soon there was no more rock left to mine. Only soil. The whole hillside had given up its rock and now there was nothing. We were all very sad because we knew what this meant. No more work for us. There would be no more food for most of us either and no more Saturday dances and no more fun.'

He paused for a breath again.

'About a week later we were all dismissed,' he said. 'The owner of the quarry could not take us along with him when he went in search of more rock unless we agreed to a fifty per cent reduction in pay. The ones among us with wives and children readily agreed. The children and wife must eat, you see. The rest of us told the Asian to go to hell with his fifty per cent and he left. He packed up his contraption and went up north in search of more rock mines. We went down to the city completely lost. Fortunately one of my miner friends knew a number of people in the city and for a time we had no difficulties. We slept in their houses at night and spent the day in one of the city roundabouts or parks. We tried for jobs with little success. A day here and the other day there, but nothing permanent. Then the friends and relatives tired of us wastrels and told us so with their eyes and actions. We had to get out fast before they used words and humiliated us. We left and went into the streets.

'My friend had other ideas in mind and now that we were all alone in the streets and had nothing better to do he put them into practice. At first we were inexperienced and frightened. But then we got used to rough living and went about twisting the law. We did almost everything it is not right to do. We picked pockets, snatched purses, cheated, robbed, everything. We fell in with gangs and went from bad to worse. Short of murder we did practically everything. My friend was brave and adventurous and he won favours among the gangsters. He led them everywhere. And,' Meja laughed uneasily, 'I was his assistant. We became very daring. We broke into houses in daylight.'

The others were very attentive now. This was the climax. The reason was approaching. The time for truth.

'That is why I am here,' Meja answered their unasked questions. 'We broke into a white man's house while he was away on leave. We practically swept the house of all its belongings. We worked at it overnight and we had even time to force the wall safes and lockers. There was little loose cash. We did not know how to get rid of the booty at one sweep so we hid it in the forest and sold it on the black market piece by piece. Unfortunately the owner of the stuff came back from leave before we had managed to do away with the lot. Somehow, I don't know how, the police caught on to our arrangements and arrested one of us. He did not only talk on us. He yelled. He told the police everything. Not that this was not to be expected of a gang member once in the hands of the police. It was just that he told them a little too much. Before we knew it we were being shadowed every moment of the day. Whatever we did was noted and there was no privacy any more. Then the great day came. On that day we were to get rid of the last batch of the booty.

'According to the plan, we arrived at a lonely forest road in the taxi that was to carry away the luggage. The market was ready and the taxi driver cared not where we went so long as the charge meter kept running. I was dressed as a rich property owner and two of our boys as labourers. So we parked by the side of the lonely road and vanished into the woods to bring out the last of our collection of household goods. What none of us suspected was that two policemen were waiting for us by the hidden goods. We turned and started running back to the taxi. When the taxi driver saw the policemen behind us he panicked and drove off. We scattered and ran in different directions. The two policemen were not to be fooled and they came after me. I could not hope to get away limping as I was, so I stopped and put up a fight. I was stronger than the two of them put together and I made short work of them. But then just as I turned to vanish into the bush a car load of policemen arrived with two huge hounds. The hounds limped me up a tree. I promised to climb down on condition that the dogs were tethered. They agreed and I climbed down. Then I wished I had included the condition that they would not beat me. They stopped beating me when I was one big ache and bundled me into the car. The dogs followed my companions but lost their track deep in the forest. They came back after a few hours and collected the rest of the baggage. We drove off to the station.'

Meja paused and noticed that the others were captured by his story. They lay on their sides, heads on elbows and stared at him.

'I was there a few days before they took me to court,' Meja went on. 'During that time they questioned me about my friends. I told them less than they expected and this did not help my health. Those beasts beat me more than I thought they would. Then the white man came to identify his property and make his statement. When I was brought face to face with him in court I had the experience of my life. The first thing he did was claim the suit I was in as his. He described even the different types of stitches it had. They checked and he was quite right. I was made to take it off. Then he had a closer look at the shirt and said it was also his. He was right again and I had to take it off as well, as material witness. I was very nervous by this time. The shoes and socks I wore were his. And so of course was the underwear. Like everything else I had to take them off. Some samaritan produced a blanket and threw it round me. Thus garbed I stood for my trial.'

He paused and let the giggles die down.

'The judge made short work of the case. I pleaded guilty as there was nothing else to plead. This pleased the judge and satisfied everybody else. He called me a few unpleasant names in the name of justice and very leniently, or so he said, gave me one and a half years for my part in the robbery. They are still looking for the others and I don't think they will ever get them. So I came here dressed in a blanket like an old scarecrow and was assigned to Number Nine.'

The listeners lay back and looked up at the roof, satisfied.

'Any questions?' Meja asked.

None spoke.

'Satisfied?'

'Satisfied,' Maina said for all. 'You have really qualified for cell nine, coming in a blanket like your ancestors.'

'He must be the first prisoner that ever came into this place in

123

only a blanket and nothing underneath,' Chege said. 'They might even enter him into the book of records.'

'The question now is how do I get out of here with no personal clothes to claim?' Meja asked them.

'And your blanket?' Maina asked.

'They took it back to the owners,' Meja said.

There was a pause.

'I will let you take mine,' Ngugi offered. 'You go out before me, so you can take mine and send it back when you get something to get into.'

'Or bring them back if you cannot afford to send them back,' another of the inmates said. 'They can always allow you back in if you come dressed in an old blanket.'

A few people in the cell laughed.

'What are you in for, Maina?' Meja asked.

'You will not believe me,' Maina told him.

'Rape?' Meja asked, guessing at the most incredible crime anyone in his right senses would think of committing.

'No,' Maina told him.

Ngugi sniggered.

'Murder?' Meja guessed again.

The older members of Number Nine started laughing.

'Not murder,' Maina said laughing lightly too.

'What is it then?'

'Stealing.'

'Stealing what?'

'Milk.'

Everybody in the cell except Meja and Maina were rolling with laughter.

'Milk?' Meja asked suspecting a joke. 'What for? How much milk?'

'Fifty, eighty pints a day for a week,' Maina told him.

'But what was it for?' Meja asked.

'My wife gave birth,' Maina said trying to look like a concerned father. 'The baby had no mouth and therefore could not suckle. I had to get some milk somehow so I stole it.'

Meja sniggered.

'And the baby that had no mouth drank fifty pints of milk a day, is that not so?' Meja said mockingly. 'How very much like the father. I will not be surprised if you tell me the baby could talk as well.'

'That is just the point,' Maina told him. 'He said he did not like the milk and I had to sell it every day. Then the inevitable police came into the scene.'

There was silence. Heads started disappearing into blankets.

124

'You have not told me for how long you were thrown in, Maina,' Meja said.

'For a year,' the other said. 'Four months remaining before I go out. I will leave you here. But don't worry. I will also find you here when I come back.'

Somebody started snoring. In the silence that reigned over the whole cell block the snoring sounded like the roar of a bulldozer in high gear. Meja turned over and lay on his side. Beside him Maina also turned.

'Switch off that machine,' he shouted to the snorer.

The snorer was too deep in sleep to hear him.

'Will somebody kick that beast into silence for me?' Maina asked.

'My pleasure,' a voice said.

There was a thud. The snorer grunted, turned on to his side and went back to sleep after mumbling a few words in sleep code. He did not snore again.

Meja sighed and covered his head with the blanket that smelt strongly of D.D.T.

The dim bulb high in the ceiling threw its light on to the covered bodies. Outside the cell the whole prison was asleep, except for the warders along the fence and on the watchtowers. Half a mile away on the highway, a vehicle honked and sped through the night towards the sleeping city.

11

FOR THREE MONTHS rain fell unceasingly, day and night from the dark sky. The stream that ran between the village and the fields was now a roaring fury and nobody dared try crossing it to go and see how the fields were taking in the water. Everybody stayed at home and the rain fell.

At first the maize fields swallowed the rainwater hungrily and the small stalks leapt up gloriously towards the cold black sky. Then as the downpour continued, small malicious tufts of weed sneaked from the soggy ground and spread their first leaves. And when the gardeners did not come to weed them out as they had anticipated, the young weeds produced their second lot of deep green leaves and waited. The rains continued and the farmers did not come and the maize grew tall and strong and the cobs started thickening. The little weeds grew bolder and shot after the maize, weakening and sometimes killing the smaller stalks. Then they matured, dropped their seeds and a new crop of young healthy weeds sprang up and they too headed for the ugly black sky. And still the farmers did not come, for the stream between the village and the fields was still swollen and dangerous to cross.

Then suddenly one morning the sky cleared and the sun came up warm and beautiful and dominated the blue sky. The stream went down rapidly as the sun continued to shine for a few days. The farmers busied themselves with the clearance of the weeds, which by now were giants fighting to choke the maize stalks. This was done in a hurry for everybody said that the rain would surely come back soon. Then the fields were clear of weed and they waited for rain. But the rain did not come back that month nor the month after that. The rain did not come back that whole year.

The maize in the garden started turning brown and the stream slowly reached its original level, then went down further until soon there was not any depth left for it to fall to and it was completely dry and thirsty. Cold dry wind blew everywhere carrying dust from place to place. The maize stalks could neither grow up further nor go back into the ground so they stood helplessly and let the wind blow them this way and that and every passing day saw them browner and browner.

In the village across the stream there were cries of anguish as eager faces looked up into the sky and saw not a cloud in the expansive blue space. In the stores outside the village huts the food dwindled. At last the village rang with the laments of the women as they put the last grains into the cooking pots.

The village witch-doctor was called to the rescue. He brought down his profession's tools from the rafters where they had long been hanging and laid them out on the black sooty carpet. Roosters were offered to the gods and then to the goddesses but still the hot globe of fire shot into the sky punctually every morning, not at all abashed by the distress it was causing all over the land. In desperation the witch-doctor folded his mat and put his instruments back in the rafters. Then with a shrug of his crooked old shoulders he lay back on his sack in the corner of the hut to give the gods time to digest what he had offered to them. Meanwhile the sun glared down on the dirty brown maize fields, hot and destructive.

The village was thrown into chaos. Everybody and everything was hungry and lean. The village committee met for the hundredth time to decide what not to do. During the meeting someone mentioned the co-operative society in the city that bought their milk and crops when harvest was good. Surely such an organisation would help during the reign of hunger. A delegation of the most respected old men was sent out to the city to ask for help. They stayed for two long weeks and everybody waited eagerly, hoping that the delay meant that they were getting food bought and prepared for shipment to the village. The delegation came back not with help but with another delegation from the city, sent to make sure the old men were not exaggerating the difficulties of the farmers. The society's delegation did not stay long. They left sincere promises that they would come back with help and were never heard of again. When they had allowed a dignified period of time to pass, the farmers sent out a second delegation to the co-operative society. The second delegation came back much sooner than the first with the news that the society had moved its offices and left no address. That was the last straw. A few people died of starvation and disappointment. Cattle and other livestock died in dozens. The pessimists sold out to the optimists and left while they could. A few other helpless souls hung on and sent an SOS to the witch-doctor.

For the second time the magic man brought down his medicine bag from the rafters and the last rooster in the village, thin and ill, was sacrificed to the gods, this time with a few extra incantations. Then he slunk out to watch the sky for any results. Far out in the east, a speck of cloud rose out of the horizon. It would be many days before that grain of cloud grew into rain. The old man shook his head sadly. He crept back into the hut and lay prone on his bed.

Outside the hut a whirlwind came down from across the stream bringing a cloud of hot dust into the village. From up above the sun smiled majestically at the desolate land below. He was much pleased by his work. Much pleased.

The long-awaited rains did come after all had given up hope. And when it came the rain fell just as hard as it had done before the great drought. The witch doctor received his pay which everybody owed him. The land was green and the livestock that had managed to survive the drought were now fat and contented. Cows struggled under the weight of their over-full udders and their calves cried with joy and stampeded with energy. Children played in the fields into the late hours of the evening and song and laughter filled the land once more. Everybody was at peace with everybody else and the gods with all. There were even rumours that the co-operative society man had been seen prowling around the green maize fields. And now that the bad times were over and done with, no one was particularly bitter about the co-operative men.

And it was during this season of beauty and plenty that Maina came back to his home village after being away for more than ten years.

The sun was about to set and darkness was closing in. The western sky was tinged gold and a cold wind blew strongly throughout the bush and the countryside. Above the village rain-clouds gathered and every- thing on the ground below braced itself to meet the storm.

Slowly and painfully Maina laboured up the steep footpath that wound its way up the hill to the maize fields and across the stream. Although the evening was cold, sweat stood on his face from the effort of carrying his weak and broken body up the steep path. His heart was beating fast and he was breathless. Every now and then he stopped to rest and during those brief moments thought about his home and family. It had been a long time since he went out to the city to look for a job. Would his family recognise him? In that time he had changed from a boy to a man, from a man to a thief and a robber and on to a jailbird and a wreck. Would they see in his rotten body the son they had lost?

He had been so fed up by the city life that home seemed the only way out. But going home was also a nightmare. He tried to lose himself in gang life but the Razors' time too was running out fast.

Sara suddenly discovered that she was a woman not a gangster. She deserted the Razor and his temper became very bad. His blade appeared too often and he could no longer keep gang discipline. The members lost faith in his leadership. Then he took to drinking and his

128

health deteriorated. He kept raving about Sara. A few months after she left he was found in a ditch by the roadside one morning. The Razor died from alcohol poisoning.

Several men took the opportunity to try their hand at leading the leaderless gang. The Sweeper used too much force and killed a gang member when enforcing discipline one morning. He was hanged for that. The Professor tried his hand. He tried all his logic but failed completely. He went mad trying to make the one-eyed Crasher see things from his point of view, with both eyes open. They hustled the Professor off to the asylum, crying like a hurt baby. More gangsters tried their luck and also failed. Maina tried and gave up after losing a fight against a rebellious gang member. Meja tried and found that he too would not get far in the career without killing one of his reluctant subjects. He gave up also, and the gang was scattered like grains of sand in a storm.

Maina's heart was now full of insecurity and hopelessness. He tried to retrace his old girl companion Delilah but without success. She was neither at the old Shanty Land nor at the new one. He even had the courage to go to the Friends' Corner but there he found a different girl and she told him that Delilah had left to be married two years earlier. And that was the last bit of hard luck. Delilah had found her man after all. So Maina slunk back to Shanty Land and into the Razor's hut, the only thing that remained from the good old days.

His friends found him dangling from a rope fastened at the highest point of the roof. They cut him down, and since he still had some life left in him they worked on him until he could speak again. They were all very sorry about their friend's failure of courage and they told him so.

'It is not that,' Maina told them in a halting voice. 'You just cannot understand. It is . . . it is . . .'

'We understand,' someone told him. 'We understand very well. You are tired of going back to prison. But that is very little matter. We shall all be together. Do not be afraid . . .'

Maina shook his head.

'I am not afraid of anything,' he told them. 'I have done almost everything in this world. I have committed all crimes you can think of and been jailed for most of them. I have been in prison more hours than I have been out of it within the last five years. While I was in I dreamed of lots of things I had not done. And when I went out I did those things and went behind bars again. I am just sick and tired of this. I mean, where does it all lead to? I am not being of any help to anyone now, am I?'

The gang was for a moment quiet.

129

'Yes, you are,' one of the gang members told him. 'Your people. Your mother. Your father.'

Maina glanced at the speaker and shook his head.

'No, not those,' he said slowly. 'To them I am dead. I will go anywhere but not back there.'

'Doesn't anybody like you?' the other asked him. 'We like you here but what about back home, don't even your parents love you?'

Maina sighed. The rest of the gang kept still.

'They love me,' he said thoughtfully and his head hammered its protest at the memories.

'Don't you like them?' another of the gang asked.

Maina shook his head to clear away the old memories.

'I love them,' he drawled staring at nothing. 'Yes, I love them. I love them too much. That is why I will not try going back there. I should not. I must not.'

There was a pause in the talk in the small hut in the middle of Shanty Land. In the gloom everybody watched the sorrowing figure and shook his head. Only one man did not look. This man sat quietly listening to what the others were saying and staring at his crooked right hand. He just sat seemingly indifferent and stared at the scar, thinking. Every now and then he flicked a glance at the man they had just cut down from the roof.

He remembered his first meeting with Maina in the backstreets. Maina was different then, a young man with a certificate of education, full of fun, and determined to go on living against the odds. Maina did not seem in the least suicidal then. He had talked full of ideas and hopes for a future. It was he who had prevented his friend from giving up living. And here he was the same man, the same teacher now desperately trying to die.

Meja shook his head.

'You can stay with us here, Maina,' someone said.

Meja looked up quickly.

'No, he should not,' he said.

The others were startled. They stared at Meja agape and waited for an explanation.

'He really should not,' Meja told them in general. 'He has not said he lacks someone to stay with, has he? His problems run deeper than any of you think. He can't explain either and therefore no one can help him. He will not be satisfied merely by staying with his friends.'

He threw the rope at Maina.

'There,' he said. 'Go hang yourself. That will satisfy you. Go get it done with. Only do not string yourself in our hut. Go now. Get out.'

The gang watched open-mouthed with horror. Some tried to speak but Meja stopped them with a wave of his hand. And his hand carried a lot of authority being the most muscular in the dark hut.

'Go hang yourself and die, Maina,' he said bitterly. 'That should solve your sentimental problems. If it does not solve them you will be dead anyway and it will not matter then. Go die. There is no place for cowards in this world. Get out of here.'

The hut held its breath and fear, anger and confusion hovered among them.

Maina looked at the rope at his feet and then at the gang and Meja. He stared at Meja and it was clear how much he had been disturbed. In place of the desperation that had weighed him down, he now felt an overwhelming bewilderment. He opened his mouth to say something and closed it leaving whatever he had wanted to say unsaid. Then he understood. It was a challenge. He nodded, picked up the rope they had removed from round his neck a moment ago and nodded again. He started for the door.

Everybody else watched, some with tears in their eyes.

'And, Maina,' Meja called.

The other stopped and stood fingering the rope.

'Make sure the knot is tight enough,' Meja said. 'It would be sad if someone else pulled you down by mistake the way we did.'

Maina glanced back and nodded. Then he turned and was gone.

A gang member jumped up to follow but Meja barred the way.

'Out of my way, you . . .' the man started to say.

'Nobody will disturb him,' Meja said slowly. 'This is his private battle with life. He has not asked for any assistance. He must face it alone, and nobody is to bother him. Leave him alone. Go sit back where you were.'

'But . . .' the other complained.

'You swine,' another gang member called. 'You don't care about the other people. You only . . .'

Meja looked round at the speaker.

'Maina is not your brother,' he said. 'Don't get excited now. You will never miss him. You will forget him faster than you want to make the others think. So will everybody.'

He excluded only himself from the 'everybody'.

'Nobody made any fuss about the Razor's death,' he reminded them. 'What is so different about Maina?'

'If he hangs himself, I'll . . .'

Meja shook his head.

'You will not hang yourself too, will you?' he asked.

Nobody answered him. Some of them were already beginning to see what he was driving at.

'Maina will not hang himself,' he told them. 'He is too good for that. He will not go home either.'

'But what will he do without us his friends? Where can he go?'

Meja shook his head again.

'I don't know,' he said thoughtfully. 'But he will not go back home. That I am very sure of.'

That was where Meja was wrong. Maina had been so embittered by his friend's attack on him that he felt he hated him more than life itself. Maina was not one to be pushed into the grave by a squabble. He was going to show them that he was not an outcast. That was a personal challenge. He was going to go right back home, and unlike Meja, he would go all the way. He would not turn back as Meja had done. He was going right back to his people to tell them to kill him themselves if they did not want him. So he footed the thirty miles from the city to his home village.

But now as he climbed the steep path leading to his home, his courage started to lag behind. His conscience lagged behind too. It did not want to go back home with him. His weak body and hungry stomach pushed him expectantly up the path towards home, where rest and satisfaction awaited him; but his mind could not overcome the barriers between him and his people. What would he say? What would they say and what would they do? And then what would he do?

Halfway up the path he stopped to get back his breath. His head raced on ahead of him and went through his past from leaving home, all through to arriving home again. He thought a great many things.

He looked up at the gathering storm above him. It would soon rain. He looked too at his thin limbs and ragged clothes and shook his head.

'I hope they recognise me,' he said shivering slightly. 'I hope they have a fire too.'

He started climbing again and reached the top of the hill as darkness covered the village. He stumbled through the maize fields and used what he could remember of his earlier knowledge of the paths that criss-crossed their way through it, the paths he used to walk with his eyes closed when a small boy. He waded through the stream and found his way in the frightening dark. Night-birds started calling all over the countryside just as he entered the village. He searched from door to door using what landmarks he could remember. But here his memory and the dark failed him. After a fruitless search for his father's house, he knocked at the door of one of the huts. A woman opened the door and in the light of the fire burning in the hut behind her, she looked at the ragged figure. She could tell by the hungry look in his face that he was a stranger. Only a stranger could look that famished.

'Yes?' she asked him.

Maina struggled for words.

'Where is the house of Kamau?' he asked.

'Kamau?' the woman asked puzzled. 'What is his other name?'

Maina dug into his memory but he knew no other name for his father. While to other people he had always been Kamau, to Maina he had always been father.

'He is Kamau. My father,' he said hysterically.

'I don't know him,' the woman said.

Maina became desperate. He shouted at her and shook one thin fist in her face. She retreated and slammed the door shut. For a moment, Maina stood with folded fists and gnashed his teeth. He felt like going in after her through the closed door but his body could not allow him. It was too weak for that. He dragged himself to the next hut in line. Total darkness now covered the whole village and the wind was wailing. The first peal of thunder shook the night just as he raised his hand to knock on the door of the hut. A man came to the door.

'Where is the house of Kamau?' Maina asked hesitatingly.

'Which Kamau?' the man asked covering his hairy chest from the cold wind.

'I . . . Kamau,' Maina said. 'They called him just that. He is my father. Kamau. Kamau. That is his name.'

The man regarded the pathetic figure for a moment. Then he shook his head.

'You know him,' Maina told him desperately. 'You know him. He is my father. Kamau.'

'There are many Kamaus out here,' the man told him. 'There is Kamau the father of Maina and . . .'

'That is him,' Maina shouted. 'I am Maina. Where is he, where is my father?'

Just then a flash of lightning cut across the dark night and illuminated the puzzled look on the other man's face. He looked Maina up and down twice then shook his head.

'Are you Maina?' he enquired.

'Yes, I am Maina,' the other said. 'My father's son.'

'Are you . . . are you the one that went to school?' the man asked.

'Yes,' Maina said and nodded.

In the little light that managed to find its way round him he looked Maina up and down again, then shook his head. Maina then realised the significance of the question and his heart contracted painfully. His legs trembled, his face felt hot and his head started aching. Rage welled up in him and he hated the man who stood in front of him, laughing at him. To his mind there was only one meaning to the other's astonishment. The man was laughing at him because he went to school and was dressed in rags. And Maina hated him.

'Where is my father's house, you pig?' Maina hissed through his closed teeth.

The man shook his head, opened his mouth to speak then closed it.

'Where is it?' Maina snarled.

'That one . . . over there,' he said and banged the door shut.

Maina staggered into the night in search of the house he was directed to. A high fence ran all round the hut. The door into the compound when he eventually found it was closed and bolted from the inside. He stood at the door, his heart racing with ecstasy at coming back home. Now that he was right there at the door he was again not sure he wanted to see his people. What if they took the same attitude as the neighbours? What would he say, where would he go???

A dog barked from behind the high fence. His stomach contracted painfully. He knocked on the closed door. The dog behind the door raved. In desperation he banged on the door harder and shouted.

'Father, father, mother.'

The door opened slightly and someone looked round it. Another sword of lightning cut across the dark night and for a moment Maina saw the face of the man behind the door. It was neither that of his father nor of anyone he could remember. The face also was confused for this was not the hour and the weather in which neighbours called on one another.

'Who are you?' the man asked.

'I am Maina.'

'What do you want?'

'I want my father, Kamau,' Maina said. 'I am his son.'

The man hesitated. Maina noticed this.

'What . . . is this not the house of Kamau, my father?' he asked.

The man sighed.

'He doesn't live here any more,' he said.

Maina's body grew numb and a whirlwind of theories and tragedies swept through his mind. His throat constricted so that he could hardly breathe.

'What . . .?' he asked.

The man shrugged.

'I am new here,' he said. 'I have just heard stories.'

'What stories?' Maina asked.

'Well, they say that the family was poor,' he said, sounding very reluctant to retell the sorrowful tale. 'They squandered all their money on sending one of the boys to school. The boy read well, so I hear. He was the good type. But when he finished school, he went to the city, got himself a job and became spoilt. He never came back.'

Maina dug his nails into the wood of the door-frame. His head ached and his body trembled. His breath came out in a low painful whistle. His mind whirled faster than he could follow round and it was all he could do to stop from collapsing.

'During the time of the long drought,' the man went on, 'the old man sent his remaining sons out to the city to look for the lost one. They too never came back. That old man was clever. And his wife too. Those two were good people. Well, the drought got worse and his old woman fell ill from worry. The old man sold out and went away with her. Just the two of them. I bought this place and ... you said you are his son?'

Maina nodded in the dark.

'Do you know where they went to?' he asked.

'He just left,' the man said. 'Not a word to anyone.'

Maina's head whirled faster. The new owner of his father's property saw him sway.

'Would you like to come in?' he asked. 'It is cold out here.'

But Maina would never enter that hut again. Not the hut he was born in, brought up in ... the same hut in which he had left his father. Never again.

He turned round and started back the way he had come. The door banged shut behind him and the dog started barking again. He stumbled on in the dark, oblivious of the cold wind raging around him. Stinging hot tears ran down his cheeks. He had no idea where he was going nor did he care.

Then the storm fell. The thunder rolled, lightning flashed, and sharp drops of rain pelted his body. He staggered, fell and for a moment lay there on the wet grass, cold and hungry and broken. And the rain fell.

He woke up minutes later to find that the rain was still falling. His whole body was now wet and his head ached with a painful throbbing sound. When lightning flashed again he saw a hut only a few yards away from where he lay on the wet grass. His head still in a daze he crawled to the door of the hut and supported himself to his feet with its frame. He knocked on it and stood waiting for it to open. He wanted food, a fire and a place to sleep. He knocked on the door harder and waited, his teeth clicking and his head one heavy ache.

There was rustling within the hut.

'Who is it?' a voice asked, faintly audible above the roar of the rain.

'It is I,' Maina said. 'Open.'

He rapped again urgently and moved closer to the door away from the rain.

There was whispering inside the hut. Someone moved within, the door opened a crack and a face peered round it.

'What do you want?' a man's voice asked.

Maina's voice failed him.

'I . . . I want,' he said. 'I am cold and hungry. Please help.'

The dark face regarded him for a time.

'It is very late,' the man told him. 'We were going to sleep. Who are you? Where do you come from?'

Maina struggled with his thoughts.

The door started closing slowly and surreptitiously.

Even with his dulled senses Maina noticed it. The hunger, the cold, the ache in his head and the will to live possessed him. He threw himself against the closing door, the owner of the hut let out a startled cry and fell back into the hut. Then he stood up and closed in on the intruder.

Maina fought like a desperate beast, with all the strength he had remaining. In his mind there was only desperation, the will to live, terror, and yes, a little anger. He kept up a growl like that of a trapped animal as he hit this way and that, frothing at the mouth and with his eyes closed.

The two fighting men upset chairs, crockery and everything that stood in their way. They rolled into and out of the still hot fireplace and all over the hut.

Outside the hut, lightning flashed viciously, thunder roared defiance and the storm poured ceaselessly from the angry sky. The dog at the house that once belonged to Kamau, Maina's father, wailed a long heart-chilling wail that faintly carried into the huts of the neighbours.

12

THE GREEN VAN turned away from the main road and drove along the dust road leading to the prison. It was late in the afternoon and the driver feeling hot and tired disregarded the thirty miles per hour speed limit. He sped along the drive and a cloud of dust hung undecidedly in the air behind the truck, until the cool mountain breeze came and pushed it down the hill into the forest. At the heavily built gates half a mile further on the van stopped, the gates were thrown open, and the driver turned into the inner compound. Over at the office he stopped, jumped out of the cab, stretched himself and yawned lazily.

The aged Chief Warder saw the prison van come and watched the usual driver step out. He watched the van and its driver for a moment wondering what they had brought him this time. He bet with himself which one of his usual boys the van had brought back, then walked out of the office to find out. He walked slowly, deliberately slowly, to the van driver.

The prisoners were going for supper before being locked up for the night and they stopped to watch the door of the van expectantly. The driver of the van lit himself a fat cigarette and stood leaning on the bonnet smoking and watching the prisoners. Then the Chief Warder shuffled out of the small office and he turned to face him.

'Another load of public headache?' the Chief Warder asked.

The driver shook his head.

'Nothing new,' he said. 'One of your usual boys.'

The old man wondered even more who it was.

'Why don't you keep them here permanently?' the driver said to him. 'I have a feeling that some of them would thank you for it. I am tired of bringing them back every other week.'

'You should leave them out there then,' the Chief Warder said. 'You don't happen to think I like seeing them around.'

The driver shrugged and spread out his hands.

'You seem to like them,' he said.

The warder thought on that one. Some of the boys were quite likeable. Some of them he understood and liked.

'Who is it this time?' he asked.

The other blew a cloud of cigarette smoke, spat and threw away the butt of the cigarette.

'You will be surprised,' he said.

He walked round to the back of the van and pulled a bunch of keys out of his pocket. He inserted the key into the lock, turned and opened it. The prisoner jumped out immediately, stretched himself and yawned. The Chief Warder's lips parted in an amused smile. He had won his bet. The other prisoners whistled calls from the other side of the inner compound.

'Well, well,' the Chief Warder told himself. 'See who we have got back.'

'Hello, Chief,' the prisoner greeted.

The warder looked him up and down.

'Meja,' a prisoner called from the inner compound.

Meja turned and waved a scarred hand.

'I will be right over,' he shouted back.

The warder looked from Meja to the caller and back. He shook his head in wonder and Meja smiled.

'Back again?' he asked.

The other nodded smiling.

'Can't you believe your eyes?'

The warder shook his head.

Meja shrugged.

'I am here, and the name is in the files,' he said.

'What I can't understand is why you keep coming back here like that,' he said.

'A bad coin always comes back to the owner, or so they say,' the driver volunteered. 'One of your usual bad eggs, Chief?'

The prisoner spun round.

'No one asked for your wise sayings, undertaker,' he said to the driver. 'Your work is to drive that coffin of yours. Keep your mouth shut otherwise.'

The driver looked away and wrung his hands angrily.

The warder looked from one to the other and then beckoned Meja to follow. They entered the neatly kept office and Meja received back his uniform. Then as he changed, the warder started filling out forms and asking for Meja's print here and there.

'Same regulations as before?' Meja asked.

'Same as before,' the warder told him.

'Back to Number Nine?' Meja asked.

The other nodded, busily filling in a form.

'All the others back yet?'

'All but one,' the warder said. 'Put in all your fingerprints now.' He pushed the file across the table to Meja. 'You remember where to stamp them?'

Meja took the file and went through it ramming his fingerprints in it. He knew just where to put which print. He had done it often enough.

The aged Chief Warder stood back and watched him and wondered. What went wrong with these young men he could not understand. They came the first time scared and sorry for their crimes. Then it seemed they could not stop coming back. Most of them he was sure would be buried in the prisoner's cemetery when they died of old age.

'You heard what happened to your friend?' the warder asked.

Meja nodded.

'I did,' he said straightening up. 'It was in all the papers. Hard luck.'

The Chief Warder looked him in the eyes and shook his head. Whatever turned these boys into what they now were.

'You seem to enjoy being in here,' he told Meja.

'East or West, home is best,' Meja told him smiling. 'Anyway, you should be glad we like this place. Without us you would be out of work.'

The warder looked at his wrist-watch.

'You will be late for dinner,' he told him.

Meja smiled. He liked the old man more than he made evident. The old fellow was fatherly and understanding and what any person in Meja's position needed most was understanding. Each time Meja was shoved back into the prison, the old man counselled him sincerely, then always let him go in time for dinner. That was one of the many reasons Meja was never rude to him. Now he saluted smartly in the Number Nine style and headed for the door of the office.

'Meja,' the warder called after him.

Meja stopped and looked back.

'I know it sounds crazy,' the man told him, 'but have you ever thought of getting yourself run over by a car?'

Meja stood quite still. The old man sounded serious.

'No,' he said solemnly. 'Why?'

'I don't know why it crossed my mind,' the warder told him. 'I just thought it was a good idea. Why don't you try it next time you are in the city?'

'Do I look mad?' Meja asked him.

The warder shook his head negatively.

'I am going to live my life,' Meja said.

'In Number Nine?' the other asked.

'Why?' Meja asked. 'Is man not free to live where he likes, when he likes?'

'Free in cell Number Nine?'

Meja sighed, blew up his chest and stared back at the Chief Warder.

'Yes, in cell Number Nine.'

He turned to go, took a step towards the door and looked back at the Chief Warder.

'I did not mean to let you know, Chief,' he said, 'but now that you have asked I will tell you. Yes, I did get myself run over by a car once, Chief.' The smile widened into a pained grin. 'That did not stop me coming here.'

Ignoring the warning honk and screech of tyres in his head, he raised his hand and exposed the scar to the Chief Warder to admire.

'See, Chief?' he asked the wide-eyed old man.

The old man nodded.

'Yes,' he said and scratched his chin. 'I see.'

Meja walked out of the office and made for the door that led to the inner compound. The guard let him in wondering why the Chief had not escorted this particular prisoner into the corral.

Meja swaggered and limped towards the eating place. Everybody from Number Nine was glad to have him back. They clustered around him full of excitement and offered him a share of their own food. They also asked a lot of questions, most of which Meja had to make up answers for.

'Did you see my whore?' one of them asked.

'Yes,' Meja said his mouth full of food. 'What do you think I did during my spare time? I saw her more times than you would wish me to mention.'

'What did she tell you?' the other asked.

Meja smiled slyly.

'She said she never wanted to set her eyes on you again,' he said.

The other prisoner grimaced.

'You see,' Meja went on, 'she wanted to know how you were. I told her you had grown so enthusiastic about food they had promoted you to washing plates to keep you nearer to the kitchen. That was when she told me she can stand anything in the world but a cook.'

The other boys laughed.

'You are a month before schedule,' Ngugi told him.

'I know,' he said. 'I made it so.'

'What happened?' Ngugi wanted to know.

'I could no longer endure being out there without you lot,' Meja told them.

They laughed heartily.

When the meal was finished they trooped to Number Nine. Meja's clothes and bedding were packed neatly in a corner. His mates had kept their promise. He looked round the small cell and smiled. He took a deep breath, his chest expanding to its maximum. The friendly warmth round him seeped into his heart and warmed it. The carefree smiling faces and the white uniforms were a tonic. The four white-washed walls spelt freedom and security. Within these four walls of Number Nine only did he feel secure in the whole world. The food here was better than any he had eaten anywhere else in the city. And then the smiling lively faces around him. He remembered the disinterested blank looks of the faces in the city streets and shook his head.

'Are you sorry you came back?' Chege demanded.

Meja looked down and tried to hide the smile on his lips.

'If anyone tells you I am overjoyed by coming back here, he is lying to you,' he said in his saddest voice.

They started making their beds. Meja's bed was made in the usual place between the one of Chege and the vacant space that belonged to their absent friend. That was one privacy they never trespassed across. The worst crime one could be guilty of in Number Nine was occupying his friend's bed place when he was out. It was a murder case. Like blowing up a bridge while one of your companions was on the other side, alone. The only possession the inmates had in the world was that small bit of sleeping ground and taking it away was like inheriting another person's property while he was still alive. That little bit of empty floor was the only link the inmates had with their free brothers, and the Chief Warder seemed to know this. He never assigned another member to Number Nine unless the former member was reported dead or missing in action with no hope of being found again, ever.

The warder on duty came and locked them in. And like always he did not cross the doorstep. It was a sort of compromise. Prisoners in, warders out. Even inspection was done from as far away as the door. Now the peephole opened and the warder counted them. He found eight instead of seven and checked in his list. There was a plus one written in red against the usual seven marked in for Number Nine.

'Who is the new one?' he asked through the window.

Chege turned round and showed the warder his bottom.

'This is the new one,' he said.

The warder grunted, shot back the slot on the door and moved down the corridor counting noisily.

Meja shook his head at Chege.

'You boys have not grown up much, have you?' he asked him.

'No,' Chege told him. 'Have you?'

Meja screwed up his face and shook his head.

'I would not have come back here,' he said.

They got into their beds. Night came and crickets started calling all over the compound. Occasionally a car passed along the highway half a mile from the prison. And in the cell under the ever-watching dim bulb, the inmates of Number Nine lay on their mats waiting for Meja to start telling his story. As always it was hard for Meja to decide how to start telling the story. He lay back on his mat and tried choosing his words to decide where to begin.

He reached into his pocket and produced a packet of cigarettes. He lit one, puffed twice and passed it to Chege. Chege took two puffs too, and passed the cigarette on. Everyone knew the rules of smoking. No one was allowed more than two puffs at a time. That was very selfish and extravagant. Cigarettes did not emerge from cracks in the cell wall.

'Meja,' someone called.

Meja turned his head in the direction of the caller.

'You haven't told us yet,' he was reminded.

'Told you what?'

'What is it this time?'

Meja remembered the duty he owed the cell. He had nearly forgotten.

'Same as before,' he said, trying to sound careless about it.

'What did you take this time?' Chege asked.

Everybody held his breath. Meja hesitated.

'A good number of things,' he said simply.

Chege sighed and everybody relaxed. Meja felt the change in atmosphere.

'What did you expect?' he asked them. 'Treason?'

'Well,' Chege shrugged, 'you always talked about banks and money that lay useless within their vaults before you left. I thought maybe . . .' he shrugged again.

Meja shook his head at the others sad imaginations.

'Why don't you try holding up a bank yourself?' he asked. 'They would arrest you for trespassing before you reached the counters. I am no fool to go looking for such a thing.'

There was silence for a time.

'That would have made no difference,' Chege said to him. 'You were coming back here sooner or later anyway.'

Meja sniggered uneasily.

'Every time I come back here I first give them a real reason for wanting to throw me back in,' he said.

There was a pause before someone from the other corner of the cell spoke.

'Cowards cannot hold up banks,' he said.

Meja sat up slowly and looked at the speaker, a savage smile slightly playing at his lips.

'Was that your voice, Gitoore?' he asked, calling the other by his nickname.

'Yes,' Gitoore said. 'And I speak from experience. I held up a bank all alone, by myself and using a toy gun.'

'You told us that many times before,' Meja told him.

142

'When I leave this dump I will be the richest man in the world,' the other said.

Meja laughed lightly.

'No, my friend,' he said. 'You are going to be the poorest, most heart-broken thief that ever saw the inside of a prison. You should have known better than to bury your money in the public park.'

Gitoore flew up to his feet, his eyes blazing fury.

'What?' he screamed. 'You have . . .'

Meja shook his head.

'No, not me,' he said. 'The park people found it. And do you want to know what they were doing and laugh? They were digging a sewer. It was in the newspapers. "Sewer Diggers Dig Up A Fortune".'

Gitoore sat down and put his head in his hands.

'Ten years, ten years and then . . .' he moaned.

'They took the money back to the bank, the idiots,' Meja concluded.

Gitoore got back into his bed and covered his head and wept.

'They ought to let him out now that they have got back their money,' a prisoner said. 'He has suffered for nothing.'

The others were silent, and Meja's smile disappeared into a weary grin.

Chege sighed and turned from looking at Gitoore to Meja.

'What did you take, Meja?' he asked.

Meja sighed too. He was tired for he had had a tiring day at the courts with that obstinate judge.

'A number of worthless little things,' he said.

The others did not ask what as he had expected.

'I had decided to stop taking other people's property for a while after I left here,' he went on. 'I had to get something to do to keep my hands off other people's possessions. I decided to get a job.'

'And did you get it?' Ngugi asked.

'I tried to,' Meja told him. 'But all they did was look at my appearance when I hobbled in and wag their heads sadly.'

'Well?'

'So then I had to do something about my appearance,' the other went on. 'I pinched some clothes from a parked car and went to look for the job dressed smartly in them. I went to some house in the suburbs to look for any manual labour. As I stood at the door humbly waiting for an answer to my knocking, I recognised the car from which I had taken the clothes parked in the drive. Just at that moment a man opened the door and recognised his clothes in turn.'

Everybody in the cell laughed.

'I never wanted to look for a job again,' Meja went on. 'So I sold the clothes. Then I roamed about and did a few other petty things.'

'You didn't try for anything big?' Ruguaru asked.

Meja thought for a while.

'Oh, yes, I did,' he said. 'I hijacked a delivery van from the back of the supermarket.'

The others held their breaths expectantly.

'I was patrolling on my own at night,' he told them. 'The street-lamps had broken down and all I saw was a huge van parked behind the market. According to my logic, any van parked behind a super-market is a delivery van, and delivery vans carry loads of wealth. From the look of it the van was overloaded. It was lying low on the ground under the weight of the goods it held. I thought I had hit on something big. All I had to do was open the door, somehow, and take my helping of whatever was within. There was no one in sight and that was a blessing. Then I stopped. Steady, old boy, I told myself. In for a crown, in for a pound. Well, why not take the whole load and grow rich quick. I knew how to drive tractors once a long time ago and tractors are not much different from oversized vans. This was my chance to make use of the knowledge. It took me a few seconds to open the door of the cab. Doors are much the same whether on the front of large mansions or on vans. I drove through stop signs and all but made it to about thirty miles out of the city without any mishap. I parked in the bush and waited for daylight.'

He paused and his smile widened and the others waited patiently.

'When dawn came I was wide awake. I had not slept for excitement. I wanted to know how rich I was right there and then. I knew a score of places we used for getting rid of hot goods. So as the birds were beginning to sing I crept out of the cold cab like a big cat, yawned richly and started for the back of the truck. One look at the back of the truck started me hiking for the city, my goods uninspected. It was a municipal refuse truck I had pinched. Full of rubbish.'

Everybody burst into laughter and Meja laughed with them. When it was over Chege turned to Meja.

'Didn't you take any money?' he questioned.

'I did,' the other said simply. 'I am as money-mad as the rest of you.'

'How much did you take?' Ruguaru asked.

'Fifty cents,' Meja told them.

'Uh,' Ruguaru grunted.

'That was all there was in the purse I snatched,' Meja excused himself. 'And they chased me all over the town for the whole day.'

'Is that why you are here?' Ruguaru's voice was tinged with con-temptuous laughter.

'No,' Meja told him. 'They never caught me.'

'Well?'

'That is a long story,' Meja told them.

'We are in no hurry,' Ngugi said. 'I am going to be here for the next three months.'

'If you say so,' Meja told them, 'I will tell you. I was drifting along the high street when a man passed by me and dropped a ten shilling note accidentally. Swiftly as I was taught to do, I picked it up hoping no one would see, but as I looked up there were at least ten people looking to see what I would do. I had no choice but do what they expected me to do. I shouted at the owner for all to hear, and wearing my most honest look handed his money back to him. He thanked me nicely and put the money back into his pocket and patted it lovingly. Then he smiled intelligently and walked into the crowd. I was annoyed and let down, so I followed him down the street and picked his pocket.'

'He caught you?' Ruguaru asked.

'Don't be so pessimistic,' Meja told him. 'He did not. Neither did anyone else. I was very rich with the ten shillings so I decided to celebrate the occasion. I bought myself a bottle of Nubian Gin and got dirty drunk. I walked through the city feeling like the mayor and broke a few shop windows. And no one dared stop me or I would smash them up very bad. Then I met a man walking a dog and he was daring enough to stop. I told him who I was and my father's name and urinated into the dog's mouth. Then I realised the man was a policeman and the . . . the dog was a police dog. I sobered up immediately and tried to run. I did not get far.'

Everyone in the cell laughed. They sat back listening intently.

'And of course I pleaded not guilty,' Meja said. 'How the hell could I have known the man was a policeman? But the judge was not listening to my side of the story. He sent me into custody for three weeks. Three weeks in another cell but Number Nine is a long time. I could not stand it and I escaped. For two days I went into hiding in Shanty Land. On the third day I met an old friend of mine and he invited me to celebrate his first full year since he was released from prison. I agreed. It was good for settling my jittery nerves. He procured a bottle of good old gin and we sang over it. We had a fight before we parted in good comradeship and I went into the streets again. Once more I was the mayor and I sang loud for all to hear.'

'And got into another argument with a police dog?' Ngugi asked.

'Not again,' Meja said to him. 'If I had seen any mongrel at all, I am sure I would have sobered up. Anyway, there was no accident of any sort this time. I roamed and shouted until I became weary and hoarse. I could hardly limp along. I stopped a car and asked for a lift. Where to? To hell, or any place the owner of the vehicle damned well liked. Surprisingly the owner did not even argue. He gave me a lift all right.'

'To where?' Chege asked.

'Where would you guess?' Meja smiled at the dim bulb above. 'It was a police patrol car.'

The whole cell was awake and laughing. Some of the old bhang smokers started coughing uncontrollably.

'Well?' Ruguaru asked still laughing.

'I did not go into another custody,' Meja said. 'I came back to old Number Nine.'

'For how long are you going to be here?' the other asked.

'One very, very long year,' Meja answered. 'Escaping from custody is no easy sin.'

There was silence for a time. Some of the prisoners thought about their own sentences and became sad. These, turning on their sides, tried to sleep. The others lay looking up at the watchful dim bulb above them.

'I will be leaving next month,' a voice said muffled by the blanket.

'Will you remember to bring me a bottle of gin when you come back?' another asked.

'What gives you the idea that I will ever come back here after this?' the first voice asked.

Ruguaru laughed.

'Between here and hell there is no other place you devils could get sanctuary, even temporarily.'

'Not for me alone,' the other prisoner said. 'What is good for me is more than good for you. You drunkards and thieves and rapists have more than earned yourselves the privilege of seeing the inside of the devil's den. Tell you what, when I get out of here I am going straight. I will never let my fingers stray into other peoples property ever.'

Chege laughed.

'What will you bet me?' he asked.

'An honest friend,' the other said. 'He is as hard to come by as it is to keep out of this wretched place.'

Others settled down.

'The last thing I will do if ever I leave this hell,' Meja volunteered, 'will be to remember you half-twits. Neither shall I ever dream of coming back here while you are here. You see, I have my head tightened the right way round, left to right.'

'Nuts are tightened in the same direction,' Chege offered.

Some of the other inmates laughed, but none could beat Chege who let out a wild howl then farted loudly. The laughter increased.

There were the firm footsteps of the warder on duty coming along the corridor. Silence descended on Number Nine as the peephole was opened. One big bloodshot eye took in everything in the cell. No sign of a riot. No sign of anyone trying to break out either.

'Shut up in there,' he shouted. 'Is this a cell or an asylum?'

There was a pause.

'Both,' a meek piping voice spoke from the depths of a blanket.

No one laughed.

The warder cursed and the big bloodshot eye swept the cell again. All in order at a quarter to midnight. The eye retreated and the slot shot back.

Ngugi got up and went to relieve himself into the bucket in the corner of the cell. He yawned sleepily and walked back to his blankets. He glanced at the empty sleeping place that belonged to Maina.

'I wonder what is keeping Maina out,' he said. 'He was due in a few weeks back.'

Meja's heart leapt and his breath strangled him. So they did not know after all. The Chief Warder had not told them. Meja wondered whether he should tell them or leave them to find out on their own. He lay on his back staring up at the dim electric eye above, thinking.

'You have not heard then?' he asked still looking up.

'Heard what?' Chege asked.

'About Maina,' Meja told them.

'He got married to that fat cow of his at last?' someone said.

Meja shook his head.

The others sniggered.

'He got a job?' Chege said and the others laughed.

'No, you are all wrong,' Ngugi told them. 'I will tell you what. Maina has been elected his highness honourable mayor of Shanty Land.'

The others howled with laughter at the thought of Shanty Land being made city. A city within a city. A city with a difference. And Maina of all the crooks in crookland being made the mayor.

Then they noticed that Meja was not laughing with them as he should have. He just lay on his back and stared at the bulb under the roof, a pained look on his face. Tears welled in his big eyes. They stopped laughing and sat up in their beds watching him. None of them had ever seen Meja cry and a man of Meja's kind did not cry for nothing.

'Is . . . is he dead,' Ruguaru asked, a lump in his throat. 'Did he hang himself after all?'

Meja shook his head and remembered giving Maina a rope to hang himself.

'No, Maina did not hang himself,' he said to the others. He fought to hold back the shuddering sobs and keep his voice calm. 'Maina was too good to hang himself. He went home instead. He did, after he had sworn to me he would never go back there. I made him go and he did.'

The others held their breath.

'He killed two people there,' Meja said and sighed.

147

'Who were they?' Ruguaru choked on the question.

'Man and wife,' Meja said. 'It was in all the papers. They caught him fifteen miles from the village and arrested him the following morning. He was still wet, muddy and blood covered. And . . . and he was still running. Maina had a spirit.'

There was a great silence in the cell. The whole cell, even the walls and the dim light bulb was shocked into unnatural stillness.

'Why did he do it?' Chege asked. 'Maina was not a murderer.'

Meja sighed.

'He was not,' he agreed. 'He has not said anything yet. He can't. He has lost his memory and his voice. The police cannot get a word out of him and the papers said that he was mad.'

'Mad?' two people spoke together.

'That is what the newspapers said,' Meja told them.

The prisoners lay back too and stared up at the ceiling that ought to have been there but was not there, and questions that ought to have been answered but had no answers passed through their minds.

'Will they hang him?' Ngugi asked.

'I don't know,' Meja said earnestly.

There was a pause.

'They don't hang madmen,' Ngugi said to all.

'Maina is not mad,' Meja said quietly.

The others looked inquiringly in his direction.

'Then why did he kill them?' Ruguaru asked.

Meja thought for any possible reason why Maina should have wanted to kill anyone.

'I don't know,' he said. 'But Maina was no murderer. I can swear that. I have known him for years. I knew him when we were in school, when we were eating from bins and . . .' At this point he remembered the backstreets life and remembered how he had caught the parcel that led to his being crippled by the speeding car.

To this minute Meja had not come to know exactly what Maina had pinched from the supermarket that had excited everybody so much as to make them chase him under a moving car.

'More than anything else, Maina had always wanted to remain clean,' he went on. 'He would rather eat from dustbins than steal. I knew him well. He would not just kill people. It is not like him to hurt anyone. I don't even understand how we came to be among criminals. I honestly don't know. We never even thought of it when we were together. It is so . . . so . . .' He shook his head painfully and the tears overflowed. He did not dry them. 'Why did this have to happen to him? They say it is fate but is it really? Is it?'

There was silence. Some of the other inmates who were very sad and yet could not dig up anything helpful to say to Meja in Maina's favour tried to fall asleep and forget about it. It was not easy. They would always miss Maina and his dirty jokes. They would forever miss his radiant smiling face in Number Nine. It was going to be very cold without him.

Meja remembered his friend, their ups and downs and the fun they had always had when together, whether in a dark wet backstreet or in a dimly lit white-washed cell. And though he did not want to take any notice of it, there was a little fear of his own conscience creeping into the chilled corners of his heart. He was afraid that maybe his telling Maina to go and hang himself had caused Maina to go and commit murder. He thought about this and trembled. He hoped they would not hang Maina. But with the sort of record he had, his chances were very slim. It was highly unlikely they would let him go free. And Maina would miss one of the things he loved most, freedom. His love for life would be very soon wasted away in some dark hanging house.

The cellmates started dozing off.

'Goodnight, Meja,' Ngugi said.

Meja grunted a reply and remembered Maina wishing him 'happy nightmares' every night before going to sleep in their little hut in the farm far out in the memories. Those were the days. He would have given anything to hear the same words said in the same tone in cell Number Nine right then. He would have paid a lot to have Maina with him in the cell with them, rather than out in some dark lonely cell waiting to be eventually hanged.

'Meja,' Chege called. 'Was that the truth you told us about Maina?'

Meja twitched and sighed heavily.

'I read from the newspapers,' he said. 'There was his picture too.'

Chege sighed. Most of the others were now asleep and snoring softly.

'It could not have been somebody else?' Chege asked, hopefully.

'No,' Meja told him. 'I know Maina.'

There was a pause.

'Did . . . did he look mad?' Chege enquired.

Meja paused to think.

'No, he did not look mad to me,' he said. 'He was . . . he just looked like Maina.'

'And will they hang him?' Chege went on.

'I said I do not know,' Meja answered quickly.

Chege sighed sadly.

'Maina was my best friend,' he said. 'We were the first two souls that ever entered Number Nine, I and him. And I liked him a lot.'

He turned over and covered his head. Meja thought he heard him sob.

Meja thought bitterly of his friend. In the newspaper headlines, flanked by two armed policemen, he had looked tired and dishevelled as though they had pulled him out of a swamp. But he did not look mad. And now they were going to hang him. Maina of the dustbins and backstreets. Innocent Maina who only knew how to laugh and smile. He was now a murderer. The newspapers had screamed so in the headlines.

Meja glanced at Maina's vacant bedding place by his side. The Chief Warder would soon send another person to fill that vacant place. But in reality that empty bedding place would never be filled. It rightfully belonged to Maina and no one else. And it would always remain a permanent dent reminding the old citizens of Number Nine of their departed comrade.

He turned over restlessly and lay on his back. The dim bulb up above he saw through clouds of tears. And instead of seeing the orange light, he saw the smiling face of his friend Maina saying, 'Somehow we have to live!'

On the highway half a mile away from cell Number Nine and its sorrow, a car honked and sped towards the sleeping city, with its tall buildings, blinking neon lights, and its unfathomable backstreets and their mysteries.